My Jim

ALSO BY NANCY RAWLES

Crawfish Dreams

Love Like Gumbo

My Jim

A NOVEL

Nancy Rawles

Crown Publishers
New York

Published in the United States by Crown Publishers, an imprint of the
Crown Publishing Group, a division of Random House, Inc., New York.
www.crownpublishing.com

Crown is a trademark and the Crown colophon is a registered
trademark of Random House, Inc.

Library of Congress Cataloging-in-Publication Data

Rawles, Nancy, 1958–

My Jim : a novel / Nancy Rawles.—1st ed.
1. African American families—Fiction. 2. Reminiscing in old age—
Fiction. 3. African American women—Fiction. 4. Grandparent and
child—Fiction. 5. Loss (Psychology)—Fiction. 6. Teenage girls—
Fiction. 7. Women slaves—Fiction. 8. Older women—Fiction.
9. Freedmen—Fiction. I. Title.

PS3568.A844M9 2004

813'.54—dc22   2004011606

ISBN 1-4000-5400-1

Printed in the United States of America

DESIGN BY LAUREN DONG

ILLUSTRATIONS BY TINA HOGGATT

10 9 8 7 6 5 4 3 2 1

First Edition

For Malaika,

so you always remember

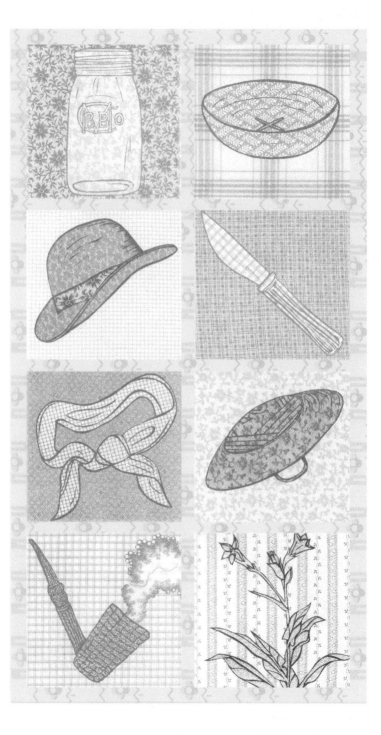

My Jim

PART ONE

Marianne
Libre

Jar

*C*has Freeman ask me to marry him.

Take me by the hand. Take me in his arms. Lift me on his horse and jump up right behind me. Show me a letter say he got duty with the Ninth Cavalry at Fort Robinson Nebraska. Got to ride out there and chase down them savage whites and Indians.

I real happy for Chas. He so proud. But I dont wants to go to Nebraska and I tells him so. Cloud come over his face and he get real quiet.

You think on it he say. Me I cant sharecrops no more. I aint born a slave and I aint gonna live like one.

Who gonna keep the land I says. But he aint got no answer.

I comes back for you Sunday after next he say. You come if you want me. You the one I wants. Chas always sure bout everything. Me I aint so sure and I cries when he leave me at Nanna Sadies cabin.

Nanna in there shucking corn.

Why you all the way crying she want to know. You ever seen a bird crying. Here you sitting free as a bird and crying like a beatdown dog. What your name she say.

You know my name I tells her.

I knows it. You the one forget. She look at me real hard cause she mad now. What your name she say again.

Marianne. I can hardly answers. Her asking make me weep.

Marianne what. She sound like a preacher on Judgment Day.

Marianne Libre.

You Free Marianne. Got a freeman asking for your hand. What you gonna say gal.

I cant says nothing so I looks down at the floor.

What year we in she want to know.

She never know the year. She say it aint important. But she know I counts the year and she make me tell her when she mad. Nanna reckon I reads and writes and figures but I aint gots no more sense than a lightning bug.

1884. I says it to my feet.

When you born gal.

1868.

How old you now.

16.

What you waiting for then.

I aint crying no more but I still cant finds my words. I hates to think bout leaving my nanna. She cant hardly see but she see my fear.

Dont worry bout me she say. Your uncles gonna come round and help me with my crop. Dont bother yourself bout me none. My spirits and my songs surrounding me.

She chewing on her pipe.

But how I knows Chas the one I asks.

He sing dont he she say. Goodlooking fella and strong. Want something for hisself. Never get with nobody dont want nothing for hisself. He sing and he know how to wear a hat. I likes a man know how to wear a hat. I bets he wearing that hat when he ask you for your hand.

She light her pipe looking at me out the corner of her eye. She see with that corner. If slaves can love you can love she say. Chas love you and he want you to marry him. I gives you two my blessing.

I aint sure I loves Chas Freeman. He almost a man but I aint through being a child.

Nanna take a long smoke. She blow heavy on her pipe.

You scared to love cause you scared to lose. You want to stay here forever. Washing white folks dirty linen. Slopping they hogs. Nursing they children.

Far as I can sees it aint so different at Fort Robinson I says. After doing all them soldiers laundry I still gots to nurse my children and slop my own hogs.

I sees you still got that tongue in your mouth Nanna say. You marry you got to watch that tongue. She put down her pipe and put down the corn. She take my hand like when I was little. She pat me on the hand.

Dont make me go Nanna. I throws my arms round her neck. We stands that way a long time till the light start to leave. We aint gots no candle and not one Liberty nickel. No oil for the lamp or Indian head penny. It summer in Shreveport and plenty hot. Moon sitting low in the sky and two of us thinking bout never seeing each other no more.

After awhile I feels my nanna crying. Aint never knows her to cry. Not even when Papa Duban die last winter. His heart fail and we finds him on the floor.

Long time ago I wants to stay she say. I wants to stay and they aint let me.

She sobbing a low moan. I tries to comfort her but she old. I cants says how old now. I helps you make the crop I says. I aint wants to leave you Nanna. They gonna take our horse and plow and chickens cause Papa Duban done sign the paper. Thats why you crying aint it Nanna.

She shake her head. Papa Duban good to me all his days she say. She move away from me. Aint love make you lose everything. Life just mean thats all.

She talking real soft now. I sees her eyes looking far away. I aint cries for Papa Duban she say. I cries thinking bout how they force me to leave my husband. How they tear my children from me. All them years ago. I wants to stay and they aint let me.

What husband I says. What children. I never hears you call they names.

My Jim she whisper. My Lizbeth. My Jonnie. Been years since I calls they names.

It so hot the door standing open. Spirits come in and fill the room with the cool of they loneliness. First Nanna Sadie rile. Then she peaceful. Singing her trance song. Rocking side to side. Her hands waving round her head.

She back in slavery days. Back fore the war. Some old people talk bout them times but they grandchildren aint want to hear it. My nanna never talk bout her captive time. I scared to trouble her bout it. She mad at me for bringing back the shame of them days. But I almost a woman and I wants to know my nannas heart. Maybe its cause she thinking I gonna leave that Nanna Sadie decide to talk. Maybe she just want to tell somebody.

She fall to the floor. I runs and gets her some water and holds the cup to her mouth. Then I takes my knife and slices a peach. I puts it under her nose and lets it rest on her lips. I calls her back to this suffering world so the spirits aint carry her off. She look at me like she seeing me for the first time.

I helps her to sit and I sits down at her feet. She rest her hand on my head.

What you recall of your mama she ask.

I picks up her pipe and takes a smoke. I draws the tobacco in deep so my throat and chest burn with it. When I talks bout my mama my throat and chest all the way burn.

Her feet in shoes I says. When she leave she got her feet in shoes walking away from me. I still hears the sound of her feet.

Nanna Sadie look tired. How long it been she say. How many years since she gone away.

8.

How old was you then.

8.

Your mama bout that same size when them Union troops come through New Roads. All the children jump and shout. Your mama follow along skipping and dancing. And some years later when them Union soldiers run out of Louisiana she follow them again. Leave you with me.

She smell like leather and dye I says. She work for the saddlemaker and he give her a old pair of shoes. One day she just walk off in them.

My Jim

Your mama born walking. You late walking Marianne Libre. Still scared to touch ground. Like the mud gonna swallow you up. It aint swallow you yet. But it hold you firm to this place. Time for you to go and your feet dont want to move. Better get you some walking shoes gal. Stop all your weeping and go on with your soldier boy. Life bound to be better in the territories. Cant be no worse. When he coming back for you.

Say he coming Sunday after next.

How many days from now.

15.

You some good at counting aint you. Lets see what else you can do. We gonna sew you a memory quilt. Cant lets you go off to no prairie less you got your family with you. They say aint nothing like that cold wind coming off the prairie.

In the heat of the day when its too hot to move we takes to sewing the quilt. I brings Nanna pieces from the gal who sew for the white seamstress. I gathers scraps from the families I takes in washing for. They say Mary you get us another gal if you running off.

Gonna back this quilt with something heavy Nanna say. Take Papa Dubans old work clothes and your mamas old apron. Gonna put something of myself in there too. Long as you got something of love to hold onto you know you a person of worth. Only folks really own theyselves the ones know what they worth.

Go get my jar she say. I gots some things I wants to show you.

They the things she keep inside a canning jar on a shelf above the stove. All these years I never knows why they there. Just a few small things you can hold in one hand. I feels them with my fingers. Knife so small. Piece of felt. Bottom of a clay bowl. Childs tooth. Shiny gold button. Corn pipe thick with tar.

I carries them things from a long time ago she say. From up the Mississippi I brings them. How old I be.

I dont know Nanna Sadie. Old as Grant I spects.

We gots to pray for the General she say. I be some sad when he go. You children cant never know what he mean to us old ones. I a grown woman fore I believes theys a white man want me to be free.

For more than a week Nanna tell me what grown folks scared to talk bout. Sometime her voice tremble sometime it shout. I listens to all she say. When she tell it in a small voice I leans close to hear. We cuts the squares and pieces our stories. I writes down everything she say.

And at the end of the telling I knows what to do.

PART TWO

Sadie Watson

Knife

Knife got blood on it. You look close you see blood. You see blood going back fore me to my mama. She take that knife when she leave Virginia and I brings it from Missouri all the way to Louisiana. Thats her knife she use for doctoring. Just like the white doctors knife but aint got no hook on it. Kind of knife proper white children use for they fruit. Mama always say she from a proper Virginia plantation with rich important whites and poor important niggers. A rich tobacco place with rolling hills and white houses. She cry to leave it. Come to Missouri as a girl carrying her mamas Congo bowl and a knife she steal from her mistress.

Knife so small I sews it in my dress. I makes a pocket with a patch of indigo and sews my things inside. I knows Mas Stevens bout to sell me. I already loss my family. Now I scared to lose my things. Dress so old and tore. Nothing but brown rags and blue patches. If I bends the wrong way I feels that knife gainst my leg. And me so thin like a stalk of cane.

They push me onto the steamer. They shove me so hard I falls down. That knife cut right into my thigh. I aint cries though. Just stuffs my skirt tween my legs to stay the blood. And bites down hard on my lip to turn my mind. Hands chain together. Rope round my waist fix me to the one in front and the one behind. Heart hurt so. Aint no salve.

My Jim standing on the levee watching them take me. Nothing he can do bout it. Just stand there and curse Mas for selling me.

Fore we parts he ask can he keep my scarf. He unwind it from my head and tear it. Then he tie it round his waist. Bind me to him with a red knot. Thats why I cant lets him go from my mind. Long years later I still believes we one day finds each other.

He try to buy me out the pen. Mas Stevens wont sell me. Aint gonna sell me to Jim or nobody in Hannibal. Cant stand the idea I might goes to my husband. I gots to be punish. Worse punishment for a nigger being sold downriver. You all the way loss then. Down south they work the life out you. Let the cane and cotton kill you then buy theyselves another.

My Jim

Jim a free man then but that aint mean nothing in Missouri. Not since they make that fugitive slave law. Any no count patroller come snatch you and sell you to slavers no matter how many papers you got. Lots of folks run off never live to tell the tale. But my Jim a seer. Thats how he make it back alive.

White folks in Hannibal favor Jim cause he find the one boy everybody believe dead and he keep the other boy from bleeding to death. White folks think Jim got power for good.

They never say that bout me. My power from the devil. I the one cause Jim to run off. Sadie she got the power over him. Wherever she go she call him to her. Put a spell on him when he still too young to know it. Black folks say it too.

But aint no spell. I buries his cord thats all. Thats the cord calling him not me. I helps him come in to this world so he mine from birth and I aint needs no spell. Your first catch all the way belong to you. Thats what my mama say.

When Jim born I aint no higher than a barrel. Still too little to work tobacco. Jim come in summer when all hands in the fields for the first picking. Tobacco leaf starting to curl and spot.

Jim the first slave born in Clear Creek so Mas Watson say he bring good luck. Jim born right after Mas Watsons second daughter. He gonna be her present when she need somebody to play with.

Everybody say Jim favor his daddy. Fore Jim born his daddy disappear. Went with one of them Murrell gang promise to take him to Quincy. Aint nothing but a gang of thieves going round promising slaves they freedom. They sell him then they kill him. Leave his body in the road.

All the time Jims mama carrying him she crazy with grief. Aint want to give Mas that baby. She do everything she can to stop Jim coming. My own mama give her the roots and the leaves but her belly get bigger all the time. She fight with Mas and the driver. Trying to get them to beat that baby out of her. Thats what my mama say. But Mas make them dig a hole for her belly. So they can beat her without killing that baby.

Baby get ready to come and all the womens busy with the picking. So Jims mama got to drag herself back to the cabins with nobody to help. She aint make it all the way. Just sit down under that white oak in the graveyard and push the baby out right there between them stones.

I hears Aunt Cora calling my name. Sadie she say go see who crying out that way. I leaves the yard and runs toward the fields. Thats when I hears Jims mama moaning with the going down pains. I finds her in the graveyard but I scared to go near. I runs back to Cora and tells her what I seen.

Lead me to where she lay Cora say. But first go bring me your mamas knife. I does what Aunt Cora tell me. I takes her by the hand and leads her to the graveyard. We leaves the children playing in the dirt.

By the time we gets there the baby already come. I cries when I sees the blood. What you crying for Cora say. All babies come in the world cover in blood. Thats the way you come too. Life a bloody business gal. Better get use to it.

Cora cant see good but she feel that baby wrap inside the cord. He aint crying or nothing. Just laying on his mamas leg. Cora feel for the cord and hold it out for me to cut. Jims mama just stare at the baby like he some kind of rag and she cant find no use for him. But Cora pick him up and put her breath inside him. She try to comfort his mama. This baby might buy your freedom one day.

If you leave him lone he be free now his mama say. She reach out to take the baby from Cora. Her hands all gummed up with juice from the tobacco leaf. Now the baby got the juice on him. He covered in blood and tar. Cora take him back from his mama. She tell me to bring her some water.

I glad for a job I can do. I aint so strong but I can tote water big as me. Us children brings the food and water to the workers in the fields. Me I mostly totes round the cabins for Cora and the sick ones. I does that and empties the slop.

So I goes gets the water like Cora tell me. When I comes back Jims mama trying to cut herself with my mamas knife. I screams when I sees the look in her eyes. I drops the water and tells Cora she got the knife. Cora hand me the baby.

Then she start slapping Jims mama hard with two hands beating her all bout the head till she drop the knife and sob.

I looks at the baby but he aint moving aint making no sound. We gonna bury him right here Cora say. Next to his mama. She gonna bawl till she dead. But both of them live. Jims mama back in the field the next week and he asleep on Coras dirt floor. My mama take me to bury the cord under the white oak tree.

Jims mama must of been hoping he die cause she aint give him no name for months. All that time the fire burning in the smokehouse make the baby cough. His mama got to keep the fire going and she all the time smell like smoke. She blow smoke on her baby cause she aint want him to live. But he find a way.

Mas Watson say the baby need a name so he can write it in his book. Jims mama look him dead in the face. I names him after his daddy run away she say. Mas look upset but he go on and write Jim in his book. This ones a good boy he say. Make up for that other one. He wait for Jims mamas cuts to heal then he sell her down river. He say that sugar cane gonna take care of her. But she die fore the boat make St. Louis.

Jim nurse at Coras tit. She the only mama he know. Cora aint got no children but she take care of everybody elses children. Her own children all die young.

She got other orphan babies in there with her. When they older they gonna work the fields. Long as Cora keep them alive till then.

My Jim

Me I takes care of Jim like a sister. When he start to walk he try to follow me to the fields. Mostly I sees him at night in Coras cabin. Time Jim born I gots a baby sister name of Jenny. I only seen her once since we was small.

I the first of my mamas children and the only one Mas let her keep. Everybody say its cause Mas Watson my daddy. But they say he Jennys daddy too and he sell her off soon as she can sweep up behind the chickens. Mas say she old enough to hold a baby and pluck a chicken she old enough to go to a family in town.

He dress her up and take her hisself. She happy cause she going for a ride. Mas take Jennys hand and she wave to us. He sit her on his lap.

Me and Jenny born in Cape Girardeau. We little girls when Mas move everybody to the place at Clear Creek near Hannibal. Missouri just become a state and Mas stake hisself a claim.

We aint never been in a boat fore that and we scared the river gods gonna get us. Me and Jenny we holds onto Mama and Cora. Mas Watson sit in front with his wife and baby. He marry right after I born and the baby come right after that. She old as me and older than Jenny but she still a baby. Cant do nothing but play and sleep and eat. Me and Jenny already know how to wash and sew.

Mas find slaves can pole a keelboat upstream in angry water. Boat pile high with people and furniture. I scared of the river all the boats and people but the polemens singing calm me down. Me and Jenny we hides when the steamboat pass. It make so much noise like the end of the world. Mama and Cora scared too. Mas Watson laugh and wave.

Our last day in the river baby reach out the boat for a dragonfly. I sees her fall in. The river sweep her downstream fore her folks realize she gone. One of them polemens catch her by the foot and pull her out the water. We come to Hannibal soon after that.

Mama take up with the man save Little Miss. She bear three more babies for him. One die of swine fever but the other two grow to be boys. Mas hire them out to the tobacco factory in town. We only sees them at Christmas. I aint knows them if I sees them again.

Jim become my brother. He stand up and walk early so he can follow me round the yard. I gives him corn to feed the chickens. He pretty like a girl. The white of his eye blue like a birds egg. Eyelashes all curl up. One fall in his eye you think he being beat he holler so loud.

All us children runs round in clothes so bare we might as well wears nothing. Jim wear clothes his mistress give him. The others aint like to see him in his clothes. They push him down in the dirt and tear them off him. I aint tries to stop them. I covets his clothes too.

Mama say Jim aint regular. He got that double sight she say. Looking forward and backward at the same time.

I cant sees what she talking bout. Jim dont want to do nothing but play. Look to me like he mighty regular that way. Specially when it come to working. Aint got no talent I can sees but running round singing a teasing song. You tell him do something he dont want to do and he fix you with a stare that can run you right through. Cora got to switch him just to make him tote water. He get the bucket and forget the water. I finds him standing on the upturn bucket reaching for some blackberries. He want the ones all the way at the top.

Jim a good size fore he come to the fields. Mas use him round the house serving and fetching. He dont know what to do in the fields. I tries to show him how to find the worms and pick them off the tobacco plants.

Emma the crew leader. She lead the work songs. She make a little song for Jim bout a boy scared of a snake getting in his pants. Emma say least Jim can sing. Thats my Jim I says. Folks laughing at him.

Mas Watson got a slave driver name of Tailor. When he still young Mas hire him out to the tailor in town. He work hard and make Mas good money. Every year Mas get a little more for his labor. But Mas got trouble keeping drivers. Last driver drink hisself to death and Mas say he never gonna hire no white driver again. He call back Tailor to drive us. Tailor drive us harder than the whites. He mad bout being call back from town. Folks say he got a wife in town. Free woman gonna buy him. But she never buy Tailor and he die a slave just like the day he born.

Mas Watson send Jim to the fields cause one of the mens sick with the gout. Tailor go hard on Jim cause he spoilt. Jim get whip if he cant keep up. Tailor work him harder than the other children. Make him run the rows carrying water on his head. Beat him if he spill any.

One day Jim aint come when they ring the bell.

Tailor say where your boy.

I pretends I aint knows who he talking bout. We been working for weeks with no break. They push us into the fields before dawn. We moves heavy like shadows. Only a string of light showing itself in the sky. Aint barely lay down and time to get up.

What boy I says.

The one you give birth to. Tailor laugh. Some the other mens laugh too. Ever since I starts to fill out they like to tease me. Mama tell them leave me be.

Jim sick she tell Tailor.

He aint sick Tailor say. He lazy. You go and tell him to tote his black ass out here.

He cant work now Mama say. He take with the fever in the night. You wait till he cure.

Mama aint look at Tailor. Just keep walking down the tobacco road.

I gonna cure him Tailor say. This gonna cure him.

My Jim

He crack his whip over Mamas back. She bend down low but aint let out a sound. Everybody else keep walking. Mama get back up and start walking too. Everybody walk but me.

I tries to move fore Tailor notice me standing there. But my feet chain to the ground.

What you looking at. Tailor fix his eyes on me. You go and get your boy. You run and fetch your Jim. So I can cures him real good.

I shakes when he talk to me. Mama narrow her eyes. I starts to run off. Tailors whip sting the back of my leg and I stumbles. I knows better than to fall. Stupid niggers I hears him spit. Whip crack again. I turns round to see Mama on her hands and knees in the dirt. I starts back to help her.

Tailor looking at me to see what I gonna do. I meets his eyes. He stomp his foot on the ground like a horse bout to charge. I runs fast as I can to the cabins.

Jim laying on his pallet. He trembling with the chills and his body wet like a man been working all day. You got to get up I tells him. You got to come show Tailor you sick.

He aint say nothing. Just moan. I puts my hand on his forehead. I hears his teeth rattling round in his head. He aint stir no matter what I says.

I been gone too long so I starts back to the fields. Tailor act like he aint seen me. They got the field fire going and he standing over it warming hisself. I goes to my row and starts in to worming. I knows he gonna hit me. I just aint knows when.

He wait till the day almost gone. We gathering our sacks and starting for the cabins.

Where you going gal.

I hears Tailors voice over my shoulder. He got two other mens with him. When I turns round they grab me and hold me down. I screams. They pull my dress over my eyes. I thinks he gonna whip me but he dont. He shake his pipe over me. Ash burn my arm and stomach. I yells so loud Mas Watson come to his window. He look out at the fields but night already falling. His eyes cant see me.

Emma help Mama pick me up. They cuss Tailor and the other mens. Them mens aint do nothing but laugh.

My body on fire. It hurt to be held. I tries to walk between Mama and Emma but I cant stops shaking. The fires in my head. I wants to take a iron to Tailor. I wants to burn his cabin down.

Put your arm round my neck Mama say. We makes you a poultice to stop the burning. Dont worry bout Tailor. I gonna put something on him. He aint never gonna bother us again.

When we gets to the cabin she rub me with witch hazel salve. She make a poultice of burdock leaves and put it on my stomach. She rub some dough in lard and linseed oil and wrap it round my arm. I sees where the whip tear open her back. Let me put some salve on you Mama. You keep quiet she say and I gonna make you some five finger tea. You best to drink it slow.

Mama work the fields all day and tend the sick all night. She barely look up when I brings her biscuit and gravy. I tries to help her with her cures but sometimes I falls asleep. She wake me up to mind the sick babies. I cares for Jim when he fall down with the ague. He talking in tongues like a body possess. Cora say he burnt up in the head. He gonna be half crazy when he wake up she say. But every morning I makes him a tea of dandelion root and Indian ginger. And every night I gives him syrup from the bark of a river ash. Fore long he get better.

When Jim come to he can see. Not ordinary things but things nobody else can see. Cora say he born with the veil. But I aint remember him born with nothing but a cord round his neck.

He tell everybody a great water coming to take the living and the dead. That fall the river flood so bad half the town floating. Tailor in town walking near the graveyard when it happen. He seen bodies big like rotten wood drifting down Main Street and catching on horse draws. He watch it all from a tree. After the river go back down townsfolk call niggers to clean up the mess. Tailor say he stepping on bones scatter in mud. They gather the bodies and move the graveyard to higher ground.

After that Jim say the sky gonna fall. White folks laugh at him but us niggers believes. In our world the sky always falling. One cold night we in the cabins sleeping close together to stay warm. Mas Watson ring the bell and wake us up. He say come see the sky falling. We all scared to death. Not Jim. He the first one out the cabins.

Now the fever done left him he talk all the time. And grown folks listen. All us slaves comes out the cabins slowly. We walks close together holding onto each other. The night bright as day and all the stars falling from the sky. I never forgets it.

Jim take me by the hand and lead me close to the Watsons. They all wrap up in they coats. Pointing up at the sky and smiling. I never seen the Watsons so happy. They give us a taste of hot cider. Jim walk me back to the cabins. Almost time to light the fires for morning. He whisper to me that night. I loves you all my life he say. Till the sky falls again. I never forgets it.

Folks hear bout how Jim can see and they start coming to Clear Creek. He tell bout frost ruining the crops and boys falling through the ice on the river. He know bout other things too. Like when a mare gonna foal or who gonna shoot the first turkey. Tailor cant touch Jim now.

We gots winter things to do. We mends our clothes and turns over our gardens. Us womens and girls gathers to sew quilts while the mens butcher the hogs.

Jim aint with us much these days. Young Miss Watson want him with her all the time. He my Jim she tell everybody. He my nigger. Every day she want to know who she gonna marry. Aint no bigger than Jim and she asking who she gonna marry. Thats all she got to look forward to. I tells Jim to keep his mouth shut. He might can tell the weather and what the plants and animals gonna do. He might even know something bout us slaves. But he aint know nothing bout white folks and they doings.

Jim all full with hisself and he aint listening to me. He tell Miss Watson she aint gonna never marry nobody. She scream Daddy whip this nigger cause this nigger done curse me. But Mas Watson just laugh. He say thats how it gonna be since she got to take care of him in his old age. She aint need to marry. He give her Jim for a present.

I aint knows why she want Jim and not a girl to wait on her. She keep him busy taking care of her horse. He work her garden and tote her water. He sleep where the horses sleep. I aint sees him much. And when we sees each other we aint says a word. The woods the only place to talk.

The Watsons Baptists so we Baptists. They read the Bible. Mas come read the Ten Commandments to us from time to time. He tell us to obey.

We gots a slave preacher name of Stowe. He a old man too old for work. He talk good bout Moses and them Israelites so Mas Watson like him. We gots Sunday service in the smokehouse when the tobacco aint drying. Harvest time Mas Watson dont say nothing bout Jesus. We aint got souls when the tobacco curing.

Whites always telling us dont steal dont lie dont cheat.
And here they come stealing us and lying to us and cheating
us out our freedom. They beat us with the word just as sure
as they beat us with the whip.

On Saturdays when Mas meets with the Baptists in Bear
Creek we meets in the woods and dance the old religion. We
stays till Sunday morning. Mas forbid the drum so we claps
our hands to catch the spirits. Folks falling out and seeing all
manner of gods. Mama love them gatherings but I scared
when I still a girl. Aint wants to leave my body. Now thats all
I wants. I lives for the nights when unseen things can make a
old body sweat and jump.

Ever since I learns to walk I follows Mama to the woods
and open fields. We gathers roots and leaves and flowers. She
take my hand and show me the feel and shape of the things.
The heart leaf of burr seed and how the burrs stick to your
clothes. Soapweed with the white bell flower and leaf like a
long knife. Bloodroot leaves reaching up like hands. Red fruit
of the burning bush so pretty in the snow.

Look Mama say. A cardinal in a red tree. Thats good luck
Sadie. Come and smell the sassafras.

I takes in everything she do. This one for the fever. This
one for the cough. These you crush for the stomach. This a
cure for worms.

Tea from the milkweed for consumption. Wintergreen
keep the babies from coming. Sweet sap from the sycamore

help with dressing wounds. Fall root of the blue iris for poison. Butterfly weed for pleurisy. Five finger for all kind of things. Mama say five finger roots look like us slaves dancing.

One night in the woods we dancing and calling the spirits when a great light pass in the sky. It aint like the night the sky fall and Jim aint seem to know nothing bout it. Mama say its the spirits on fire. The spirits of Mama Africa. They light up the sky so we can sees them. They want us to know they coming. She say after tonight many womens gonna carry babies. These the babies gonna carry our freedom.

That night Mama come home with a fever and after that she always got some pain or sickness. She aint old but her hair start to turn and her voice barely a whisper. She go from being sturdy like a root to soft like a flower. Now when we goes to the woods I holds her arm.

One day when I aint yet grown she take me to town with her. Its my first time in Hannibal. Mas Watson got a friend with the dropsy and he want Mama to lay her hands on him. Its close to winter and Mas take us in the buggy. He talk to Mama bout his problems. I never knows Mas to have any problems. All his problems with us slaves. One die he get another. One born he got a big smile. Mama listen and speak her mind.

I crushes the snakeroot to give to Mas friend. After Mama finish her work Mas take us by the dry goods shop. He point to a bolt of fabric and tell the clerk how many yards he want.

We waits in the street outside the shop. I hears a girl scream-ing in the yard of the house next to the shop. She bout my age. She cry cause her mas beating her with a stick. Dont look Mama say. She take my hand and pull me to where I cant sees. Mas Watson come out the shop carrying some seed and the fabric and some oil for the lamps. Later he give Mama the fabric to sew us some clothes.

On the way back to Clear Creek Mama tell me the girl I seen beat was our Jenny. My sister Mas take in the wagon. We both cries a little but we wipes our eyes fore Mas can see us. She his Jenny too. But he aint crying over her.

Last I remembers of my mama we walking in the woods. We goes one Sunday early morning. No bell ringing Sunday morning. We sets out in the dark while other folks sleeping. Lots of sickness then. You can hear folks coughing and moaning in they sleep. We aint comes back to eat. We eats what we finds.

You all the way remember Sadie. Poison leaf and root for killing. Dont use it less you got to.

All day we spends together in the woods. We aint goes back till after dark. Thats the only day I ever spends with just my mama. Next Sunday she gone.

Malaria carry her off. It come through and take so many of the people. Mama try to cure herself with black snakeroot and oil from hemp seeds. I gets some bark from the burning bush and boils it down for her. I gathers some blackberry roots and leaves. She drink tobacco water. She all the way say tobacco leaf good for everything. Dressing wounds. Soothing tired eyes. Frostbite. Fore she die she say she can smell her daddys pipe again. It wake her in the night and she think he come to take her home. After she die we covers her body with the tobacco leaf. It keep the smell away.

Tailor make the box for her. He darn her clothes. Him and Mama known each other from young days. They come west together with Mas.

We puts her in the graveyard. With stones we marks the place. We lays the stones in a cross and a circle. White folks got big markers standing with letters carve by slaves. Stonecutters aint spose to read the letters just carve them. Mas Watson let us put stones on Mamas grave but she aint got no name.

Cora sing the mourning song and we all cries the song till it die away. Then we goes back to work.

My mama name Liza. She nothing but a girl when Mas Watson take her from Virginia to Missouri. She say she born the year Jefferson buy Louisiana. Thats a unlucky year for colored folks cause thats the same year white folks start talking bout going to the territories.

They leave right after the harvest. Mas daddy say it too late in the year and Mas need to wait till the spring. But he dont listen to his daddy. He think he grown and got his own mind. So they start out early one morning soon as the sun come up. Mama wearing a old coat give her by Mas mama.

Mamas family mad bout Mas stealing they Liza. Her mama cry and beg him not to take her only girl. She bring the Congo bowl and give it to her daughter. Tell her this bowl keep her safe.

Congo cross come over with the Africa people. Circle round it look like the earth. Cross in the middle with arms stretching out like a wheel. Spinning till it come home.

Center of the cross where the spirit touch down. You put whatever you want for healing right on that spot. Then you pound it till it take in the power of the bowl. Mama keep it with her all her days.

They walk cross the mountains from Lynchburg. Mas Watsons daddy give him Cora too. She young but strong like the mens. She chop wood and push a plow. Skillet ham flour lard tools salt rope bacon squash. She tote it all over the mountains. Cora can work and carry two babies at the same time. Both her twin babies die fore she leave Virginia. Mama her daughter now.

Mama say she so tired she cry when they get to Charleston. She tall but she skinny and not too strong. All that way over the mountains she carry a cask of tobacco in a sheet tie to her back. On her head she carry a kettle with jars of blackberry jam wrap in calico. Congo bowl she tie in a rag wrap round her hand. Inside the bowl she got blackberry root and columbine seeds. In her pocket she hide the knife she stole. Feet so sore from toting all them things. Load for grown womens and she aint even half grown. When they get to Charleston Cora rub her feet with garlic.

In Charleston Mas purchase six slaves. Young mens all of them. Mas Watson young hisself. He purchase him a ox cart. Mama glad to load up the cart and not have to carry nothing but her bowl. Mama and Cora sit in the cart top all Mas things. Mas sit in front with his gun. Two the young mens walk longside the ox. Other four follow behind the cart.

By the time they get to Louisville they hands burning from the cold. Mas Watson got a brother there and thats where he plan to settle. But Mas and the brother argue. Mas want to sell him the ox cart but his brother dont want it. He aint gonna pay Mas for the young mens either. Mas call his brother a thief. One of them young mens try to run off. Mas brother set the dogs on him. They leave Louisville the next morning.

Mas know a Virginian in Cape Girardeau. So he trade the ox cart for a flatboat and they start down the Ohio. He got them niggers chain together cept when they pole the boat. Even then they got chains on they feet.

Wind on the river cold and sharp. Mas Watson wearing gloves and a hat of fox fur. Cora and Mama both wrap inside Mamas new old coat. They waiting to get someplace they can build a fire. When they come upon Cairo Mama say she never so happy to see a dirty river town.

Mas dont want to stay long in Cairo. Mama say he scared he gonna lose his slaves. Somebody might put a gun on him and snatch them. But Cora say they cant walk no more. One of the men fall down. They cant drag the body with them. Mas got to unchain them so they can rest. But Mas too tired to hold his gun on them. So he pay a boy to find him a place to lock his niggers up for the night. The boy take that coin and dont come back.

Mas march them dead tired slaves over to the street below the dock. Got some men over there watching two dogs fight. They betting who gonna win. Mama say one a big dog with dirty brown hair. The other one smaller and coal black. Black dog pin the other one down and go for his throat. She so scared watching them dogs fight she soil her dress.

Mas pay the owner of the black dog to mind his niggers while he go to sleep. Fore he lay down they separate the mens from each other. Each one tied up to a post under the dock. They got to sleep standing up. Cora and Mama lay down in a crate near the black dog. All night long that dog run at the crate while his owner laugh. Him and his friends bet on who that dog gonna eat for breakfast. Mama say thats all she remember of Cairo. A dogs bloody breath and teeth.

Next morning they set out from Cairo in the dark. They walking long the banks when the earth start to thunder and everybody fall. Ground buck like a wild horse and throw them off its back. Noise so loud Mama say she know the world bout to end. Deer sliding off the bluff. Bluff falling in the river. River rising up and snatching trees. Birds and pigs screaming in fear. Mama pray. Kettle go rolling down the riverbank. Bowl go flying out her hand. Cora grab her hair and say they going home now sure. She say it in they language. River gods rising up to carry us off. We spirits now. Like the people carry off from Congo. Never seen no more till we come back in our grandchildren.

Then they hear the young mens shouting. They sliding down the banks to the river. If one go aint nothing the others can do but tumble down behind him. They all chain together. Mud gonna swallow them up every one. Mama feel sorry for them young mens. They yelling and wailing. But one of them catch onto the root of a hanging tree and they scramble back up the bank.

Mama say she never seen no white so scared as Mas Watson the day the earth tremble. He scared he gonna lose all his money. All his money in slaves. But he aint loss a one. Them young mens work for him all they days till one by one they die from the consumption. That Mississippi mud come up and choke them one by one. Only Tailor survive past his young days. And he a man hard like stone.

I aint never feels no love for the river. River stretching tween me and my freedom. Jim say the river the road to freedom. I says the river the home of the spirits. Muddy with all them bodies trying to cross over.

When the shaking and the rolling stop Mama see they all still there. She pick up her bowl and tie it to her head. It take them more than a week to make they way to Cape Girardeau. Most the time they walking in mud. They try to stay away from the wet sand. Got to step over trees all tangle together. Sometimes they walk on the trees. Fog hanging over them and people wandering round in a daze.

They pass close to a Shawnee village ruin by the quake. Indian womens singing a mourning song. Cora say it put to mind a African song her grandmama sing when she a child. All the way to Cape Girardeau she sing that mourning song. We sings it again when Mama die.

After Mama die Mas call on me to tend the sick. Babies burning with every kind of fever. Mens laying in they waste. Womens weak and heavy with what bout to be born. They work right up till they time come. Mas dont abide no womens sickness. Ones aint dying got to work. I works the fields cept when they need me in the cabins. I gets sick but I comes through.

That time we loss so many. Nobody know what come over us. Children loss they parents and parents loss they children. Bout twenty of us fore the scourge. Time all the dying done we only twelve. Mas Watson cuss all up and down the farm. Miss Watson go to town with her mama and big sister.

All us still standing works till we covered in tobacco syrup. Soon as Miss Watson gone Mas put Jim back in the fields. He bigger by then and his fingers aint so slow. It bring me comfort to see him. Say he dream bout spirits leaving they bodies but Mas Watson dont let him tell nobody. Say in his dream I stumbles but gets up again. He give me a string to wear round my ankle. Gonna tie me to the earth. He still my brother.

I makes a friend of a new gal Mas buy on a trip to St. Louis. We works side by side every day. That gal got a good heart. I never knows another like her. She the kind of friend see you with a wasting illness and give you her only piece of fatback. She cry with me bout my mama. Her own mama die when she born. Hold me close to her like she my new mama. I never forgets that gal. She name Gwen.

We together for the last of our childhood. I aint seen her leave. Mas sell her to pay a debt when the tobacco freeze. Sell her to Judge Durman. Meanest mas in the county. Gwen real pretty. Thats why he want her. Old Miss the one make Mas sell her.

After Mas sell Gwen I weak with sorrow. Mama gone and I feels all lone in the world. Emma sing but I cant follows.

Jim off working on Stone School. He work the quarry. Pick and shovel give him blisters. Bleeding hands. Heat like a furnace. River rock. Walls of huge limestone blocks. Niggers cant go to school but we helps build schools for the white children.

In Hannibal I seen them white children running barefoot. They got shoes for church and school. Day I gets shoes I gonna wear them all the time.

I keeps Mamas knife close in my pocket. And I hides the Congo bowl in Coras cabin where I sleeps. Mas give Mamas cabin to some mens he hire to get the crop in. I worries Mamas spirit gonna come looking for me and wont know where to find me.

I the last of my family on Mas Watsons place. Mama the first and I the last. I remembers how she use to beg Mas for word of her peoples in Virginia. Every year theys less and less till its only us in Missouri. Now only me. After Mama leave I aint sleeps for a year. I works all day and cries all night.

One day Mas Watson take me to town cause he got a friend been with the pox. She white as can be but pox aint know no color. Mas tell me to make a poultice to scare the marks away. I gathers the burr seed root and crushes it with some salt and leaf. I makes a paste with cornmeal and wraps it in a cheesecloth. My hands shake when I puts the paste on her cheeks. I scared if I makes a mistake they gonna take me out and beat me. Or sell me down the river. I scared if Mas Watsons friend die he gonna say I the one done kill her.

My Jim

Jim come long in the wagon. He see how scared I looks and try to get me laughing. Tell me he seen a real good life for me with lots of loving in it. That make me laugh good. First time Jim really do something for me. Fore its all the way me doing for him. But his voice getting deeper and his shoulders thicker. He getting away from his boyhood.

Mas Watson must of seen it too cause he hire Jim out to work the levee. Jim work unloading steamers. We aint sees each other much after that. Mas Watsons friend get better and we goes back to the farm. Jim stay on the waterfront. Thats when my troubles start.

Mas Watson tell Old Miss what a good job I done laying on the leaves. She say if Sadie that good send her to Mas Stevens place and see if she cant work a cure on him. They both laugh when she say that but I shaking all over.

I only seen Mas Stevens once and he aint seen me. He just come to Clear Creek when Mas say he aint really a farmer. Say he kill his horses working them too hard. A wagon pass with two long lines of niggers walking half dead behind it. Mas Stevens got a overseer name of Banes. He a poor white from town used to driving workers at the tobacco factory. He loss his job when he hit a worker with a piece of iron ore. Kill him on the spot. Man he kill name of York. York belong to Judge Durman. Judge say Banes owe him Yorks price. Say nobody gonna kill his slave but him.

We working the fields by the tobacco road when they pass. Tailor tell us not to look. We looks anyhow. They make for a sorrowful sight. Emma change what we singing from work song to mourning song. She use a verse bout Babylon that Preacher Stowe done give us. That way we lets them know we sees them.

After they pass another wagon come by. This one got Mas Stevens driving it. He white with red eyes. He whipping the horses. Cept they aint horses they people. Niggers too beat to cry. We cries for them.

Emma run for the road. Tailor go after her. Nobody know what she fixing to do. Tailor grab her arm and pull her back but he aint hit her. She fall to the ground and he leave her there. Yell at us to keep working. You aint never seen no nigger get beat he say. He shaking when he say it. From that day on I fears Mas Stevens.

More and more Mas Watson send me to work cures for the whites. That way he make more money off me. When white doctor say there aint nothing he can do white folks send for Sadie. They figure I cant makes them no worse. They cussing me all the while I tries to make them better. You stupid girl. You doing it wrong. Dont give me none of that nigger tonic. I ought to learn you some manners.

I scared all the time. I pounds seeds and roots and leaves like my mama learn me. Sometime it work. Sometime no.

Them times I waits to see if they gonna take me to jail. Saying I done poison them.

I aint gots no mind to poison no white. I aint wants that trouble. Only niggers talking bout killing ones gone mad from sorrow. Most of us wants to see white folks happy and I aint no different. When they happy they let us be. When they aint then nobody suffer like we does. They find every way to lead us to grief. So I tries my best to keep them peaceable. But most the time it aint in my power.

The other niggers want to know why I aint in the fields. Why she get to go to town. She think she something they say. Spending her time with white folks. Soon she gonna turn white and think we her slaves.

When I works the fields aint nobody by my side. Tailor hard on me cause I spending time indoors and he outside forever. He take every chance to kick and beat me. Nobody seem to mind. I aint gots no mama. I aint gots no Gwen. Cora at the cabins with the children. Jim on the waterfront. Only Emma there and she cant pay me no mind or the others give her trouble.

I grown but I aint feels grown. I feels loss with nobody to love on me. Pretty soon I looks for the white folks to call. I looks for them to call me from the fields to tend they near dead. I looks for them to take me into they houses and feed me in they kitchens.

I aint been inside much fore then. I only seen the inside of Mas Watsons house once. He call me in from the fields to tend to Old Miss. She got that chill in her body but me I aint never feels so warm. No smoke burning my eyes like in the cabins. I breathes real good in that house. They got light from the windows. Not just pinches of sun coming through the chinks.

The day Mas Watson call me to go to Mas Stevens my heart beat low in my chest. He say Mas Stevens cut hisself. White doctor cant get there in time.

I takes some wild geranium root and some leaves from the burr seed. My feet cracked from the cold but I hurries on down the road with Mas Stevens gal. I brings my knife with me. And my bowl.

We gets to the house and all the slaves lined up like somebody dead. Mas Stevens gal show me the bedroom door then she run fast down them stairs like she seen a ghost.

Mas Stevens laying up in bed with his red eyes all glassy with fever. He got a wet cloth on his forehead and his face all sweaty. When I comes in the room he turn his head to see who I be. He tap his cane on the floor for me to move closer.

I sees the blood then. He got his shirt stuff inside a wound in his stomach. Knife wound what it look like to me. Blood going purple. Like looking at a sow cut open for breach. Room smell like a stable. Like nobody done empty the slop.

My Jim

He call me to him. When I leans over to hear what he gonna say he spit in my ear. Tobacco juice. I feels his nastiness running down my neck but I aint dares touch it. Just lets it run onto my shoulder. I holds his eyes steady so he cant try nothing else.

Whats wrong nigger. You aint never seen no cut.

He got a bottle of whiskey next to his bed and a old slave woman sitting behind it.

Mas Stevens want you to put some leaf on him she say. Help him breathe better.

She look down the whole time she talking to me. Look like she made out of paper she so thin. Burnt tobacco bout to fly away. When she finish talking she look up and I sees one eye half close and the other one loose. She see me looking at her eye and turn away.

He need a poultice for his stomach I says. Give this root to the cook. Tell her pound it for a powder and send it back with a paste of milk and egg and flour. Take these leaves and wilt them by the fire. And I gonna need some soap and hot water and dandelion juice. Stack of clean linens too.

She disappear. Soon she come back with the juice.

I takes some mint from my pocket. Mas Stevens eyes close and he breathing hard. I puts the mint on his chest and backs away again.

Then I hears his voice. Dont bring your dirty hands bout me gal. You been rolling round in the dust.

I comes in from the fields Mas. I runs straight here from the fields when they tell me you hurt.

He tap his cane and the old woman appear behind him.

Take this dusty gal and wash her up he say.

I cleans my hands when the hot water come I tells her. You go and see if it ready.

She hurry away. Mas raise his cane like he fixing to strike me.

I grabs it and tries to take it from him. He tap it on the floor but nobody come. I peels his fingers from the handle one by one. Each one burning with fever but his grip still hard. He cuss me where he lay. Never take his eyes off me. He burn them red eyes into me. I feels cold all over.

I goes to touch his forehead and he grab my hand. Put his teeth on it and bite down hard. I aint dares scream but now my eyes on fire.

I grabs hold the bottle and throws some whiskey on him. He cry out in pain. Howl just like he human but I knows better. Devil gonna howl if you get the best of him. I puts the bottle to his mouth and pours it down his throat.

When the old woman come back she find me sitting in her chair. She see that something wrong but she look down. She got the water and some soap powder and paste. She carrying the fresh linen on her head. Her head slump down. I tells her put it all on the bureau.

I gots my hand in my pocket. Touching my knife.

I takes the water and dips a cloth in it. I presses it in my hands and dips it again. Whole time Mas Stevens staring at me. He looking at his teeth marks on my hand. He reach out and try to touch it. I pulls away. I cleans my wound fore I cleans his.

I tells the old woman to bring me some snakeroot.

How much you want.

Plenty to fill my bowl I says.

She make her way down the stairs.

You aint gonna poison me you black witch. What you need snakeroot for Mas Stevens say.

I makes you a salve with snakeroot to help bring the skin back together.

I wants to see everything you making he say. I aint gonna take nothing from your hand.

Why you call for me then I says.

I aint calls for no slave doctor he say. Mas Watson send you cause he aint want me to die. He like having me next door. I worth more than any overseer to him. His slaves fat and happy next to mine. He aint even got to tell you niggers he gonna sell you down river. All he got to say he gonna sell you to me. He try to laugh but he just hack.

Mas Watson a good Christian he say. Praying for the devil. Think the devil got a soul. What you think.

I says I aint studying no devil. But if I ever does I sure aint gonna pray he live. I prays he choke to death on his own venom.

He make a whistling sound when he laugh. You betta make sure the Lord hear your prayers he say. Cause if that devil live you aint want to be nowhere round.

I looks away when he say that. I gots Mamas knife in my pocket and I puts my fingers on it. That old woman aint come back and I stands there thinking I be done with him fore she do. Fixing to cut him cross the tongue. Gonna grab his nose with my hand and when he open his mouth gonna slash him real quick. I tries my best to save him I tells anybody want to know. I tries but it too late. Mas choke on his own blood.

I aint even scared bout going to jail. I cant believes a soul in the whole of Marion County gonna miss Mas Stevens. They just divide up his farm like they do when one of them die. Take it for scraps. And everybody be better off.

I gots the knife in my hand when the old woman come back with the snakeroot. She staring at me like she seen a ghost. You watch me I says as I takes a root from her hand. I cuts the root this way. Then I puts it in the water. Then I mixes in some mint to cool it off. You watch what I does. Stir that round with some sycamore bark. Cap full of whiskey. Drop of the patients blood.

She jump when I calls Mas Stevens my patient. Like I the one rule over him. Just for that moment I feels I does rule over him. Cause I the one that let him live. I could of cut him with her there. What she gonna say. She look at the floor and let me do what I wants.

I feels like one of them slaves aint got no better sense than to kill they mas. Thats how mad Mas Stevens make me. He one of them white folks aint got a soul. No light in his eyes. His house all close up too. All stale and dark. I wants to finish him off but he put something on me. I can hardly moves my hands. My fingers aching and stiff. Aint know what evil he put on me.

I takes the cloth and squeezes it out real slow. Then I dips it in the water and lays it over his wound. I takes another cloth and puts it on his face. Whole time my hand shaking with pain. And him looking up at me.

I wraps the geranium powder and the wilted burr seed leaves inside the milky dough.

I aint gonna take nothing from you he say.

I just puts the poultice on him and makes the snakeroot tea. All the while I aint says a word to him.

He call the old woman to give him his tea. He make her taste it first.

Be sure he drink it all I tells her. He got to drink it all for it to work proper. And it aint gonna work less you put in a drop of his blood.

Mas Stevens grab my arm and pull my face down close to his. This time he dont spit but just put his breath on me. You black bitch. He look at me hard like he seeing me for the first time. Red eyes all aglow. Dont you tell nobody what you seen he say.

I turns to the old woman and learns her how to pack the wound with hemp cloth and dress it with cotton batting. I tells her to watch for any sign of green or if the red get any bigger. When I goes out that room I gots a chill running from one end of my body to the other. I cant walks good. They got to cart me home in the back of a wagon.

Cora cant find nothing wrong with me. I just lays on the floor in the cabin too tired to move. After a day she try to rouse me. She kick me but I cant moves. Next thing she try throwing cold water on me. I laying there in my filth. I aint feels nothing.

At night I hears folks talking. She cure the white they say but cant cure her ownself.

After a few days Mas Watson call in the white doctor. He feel round under my dress and say aint nothing wrong. She just aint want to work. You need to give her the hickory cure he say. By that he mean the switch. They can switch me all they want but I aint gonna feel it. When Mas Stevens look at me I knows myself a dead thing. Aint no use in me getting up no more. I fears for the children I aint yet birth.

I only gets up to help Emma with her babies. I goes to where Cora sit with Emmas head in her lap. Emma laying on the floor with her water all broke. I sees the babies feet. First one then the other. I tugs on them. They dead those babies both of them. All blue. Emma wail like theys no tomorrow but I wonders why she crying. Mas Watson sore bout it too. I glad for them.

After that I starts to change. I thinks bout killing all the time. When I goes to help birth the babies I thinks of taking they cords and strangling them with it. Aint no more slaves need to be born.

Mama learn me what plants stop the babies coming.

Why you aint stop me I asks.

I tries to she say. I drinks the snakeroot tea and I rubs my parts with spiceberry oil. But you want to come real bad. Aint nothing can stop you.

One Sunday I in the woods when I sees them patrollers with one of Mas Stevens niggers. They running him behind a horse. I spects he the one stab Mas Stevens and run off to the woods. Somebody stab him and it must of been a nigger cause he aint call for the white doctor. He aint want the white folks to know he been stab by one of his own. Mas Watson think he got kick by a horse.

I feels sorry for that nigger cause I know they aint finish with him. First his overseer Banes then Mas Stevens hisself. They gonna beat him till there aint nothing more of him. He gonna rise up like smoke and they gonna beat him down again. They gonna hang him from a tree by the side of the road so all us slaves can see what happen to a nigger aint got no more sense than to stab his mas.

This knife old and rusty now. I use to think its my freedom. If I ever gets myself in a real tight bind I always gots my knife. But lifes a real tight bind and aint no easy way out. Every time hard luck happen to me I thinks it can be worse. I aint never understands I been living the worst of it all my life.

Everything I tells you happen long ago. Me I remembers it just like this morning. You want to know bout my things and why I keeps them close to me. I tells you if you listen.

No need to write it down.

Hat

Was the hat got me. Snuck up without me paying no mind. I smells somebody near. Figures its one of them smokehouse boys. Smell like crush bitter root. Old turnip greens.

He know me fore I knows him. I working in the packhouse bent over a pile of tobacco leaf when he come up behind me and squeeze my neck. I turns so fast my elbow catch his chin.

He howl a bit. I thinks he fooling but then I sees he got a fresh wound on his chin. You been in a fight. Somebody done cut you I says.

Piece of limestone done it he say. They got me working the pit when it slow on the docks. Them stone workers all the time want to fight. They want a fight I gives them one. Me and them dock workers we whips them good.

You sitting up on them docks drinking corn licker. Make you want to fight.

He give me his smile and I knows him then. A foot taller and a yard wider. Every bit a man now. I still thinking he my little brother. But he a man now and he got a hat.

White mans hat. Hat like a bowl. Brown with a yellow sash. No hat for a nigger. Not a free colored either. I wants to say take off that hat fore they catch you boy. But he so beautiful I aint gots no words for it. Me already grown but him still growing. I aint wants nothing to do with him.

Where you find that hat I says. I believes he stole it off a dead man or kill somebody and take it. When I studies a man I wonders who he kill to get what he got. I sees Jim in that hat with his head so high. Maybe they coming for him. I looks down the road but I aint sees horses and I aint hears dogs. And him just standing there smiling like he know better.

I buys this hat with my own money he say real proud.

Then you a fool I says. You need to save your money to buy your freedom.

I wants to look spectable.

You a spectacle all right. You think white folks gonna respect you cause you got a pretty hat on your head. Hat like that aint spose to be wore with no bare feet.

He laugh.

What you doing back this way I says. Aint no holiday.

I comes back to stay.

Then you best start sorting this tobacco I says. We aint spose to be talking in here. Tailor catch you he whip you.

I aint scared of Tailor he say. Miss Watson call me back.

What she want with you.

She want me to drive her to town. I gonna drive Miss wherever she want to go. And when she aint want to go nowhere I works in the fields. Right next to my sweet Sadie.

You sure thats all she want.

Everybody say Miss Watson take Jim so she can play with him. I aint never asks him. But I knows theys children forced to please they mas or miss. Jim aint never tell me.

He come up behind me and put his arms round my middle. Rest his head on my back. Kiss me on the back of my neck.

I throws him off.

I aint never loves no man. I aint never loves my father. No man done ever treat me gentle. I stays away from them. I dont wants they babies.

I already stops three babies from coming. I gives birth to them when they aint nothing but tiny gourds. All wrinkles and twists. I dont loves the mens who give them to me. But I cant protects my ownself in the fields. Any man want to come up behind me aint nothing I does can stop him. Mas want all the babies. Thats how he number his riches.

I tries to fight them at first. I bites they hands that cover my mouth. I kicks they legs out. But that aint stop them from coming at me.

Tailor act like he aint see none of it. He still sore bout the time I pulls my knife on him.

Jim aint know all that. He look at me and see something he want. And I wants him too. I wants his hat. But I aint wants his babies.

I needs a place to sleep he say.

You got friends. Go sleep with them.

Aint gots friends round here no more. My friends all down on the riverfront.

I sees he sad from missing his life in town. I missing my life too. Time he leave my life fall down.

He laugh when I throws him off.

Inside I so glad he come back. Glad he come back to me. But I scared to show it. They might take him away again.

He take me walking that night. I can smells the tobacco flowers. He look pretty with moonlight shining on his cheek.

I sees him that way still. A old woman me and him still a young man. Moonlight shining on his cheek.

From that day on I never sees him without that hat. When Miss Watson be mad at him and send him to the field he never take it off. Tailor knock it off. Jim put it back on. Tailor whip him over that hat but he put it back on. He think he too good for us the others say. He think he cant be whip cause he belong to Miss Watson.

The days he with her I dont sees him much. When he in the fields I sees him with his crew but I scared to look. Scared he wont be there when I looks again.

I sees him at night. Sometimes we goes courting in the woods. One night we stays till morning. Come back cover in blackberry juice. He gonna carry me off to freedom he say and never let me go. He sleeping with me and everybody know it. The other mens leave me lone.

We stays with Cora and the babies. We gots to be real quiet. Since Cora cant see hardly nothing she hear every little thing.

At first I lets him kiss me. I aint sleeps with nobody since Mama die. Since Mas sell my friend Gwen. It feel good having somebody warm gainst me. And his hands strong and hard like mine. He rub my shoulders and loose the sore of the fields. I finds myself getting ornery when he smile at another gal.

You been kissing gals at the docks I says.

He laugh.

You been kissing white gals I says.

Gal so white she might be white he say. Cant know for sure.

I aint wants you kissing me no more I says. You gonna leave me for some yellow gal.

I aint gonna leave you for nobody. You the only one I wants to kiss.

He sound real serious.

Tell me bout the other gals I says.

He lay back with his hands behind his head. Let me see he say.

Theys a gal come to market every day for her mistress. If she find me there she kiss me. From the time I just a boy she looking for me. I aint likes her at first and the other boys tease me. But when I gets a little older I starts looking for her too. She wear a hat that gal. Straw with a fat green ribbon. Her mistress give it to her one Christmas.

He lay real still.

One day not long ago I seen her boarding a steamer he say. Chain round her leg. Belly big with child. They say she throw herself in the river fore they make Cairo. They say she big with a baby for her mas. Her mistress done sell her away.

I aint wants to hear no more I says. We holds hands and he fall asleep. Take me a long time to sleep. I thinking on that gal. I thinks on her a long time fore I falls asleep. I wakes up in a sweat.

I looks at Jim still sleeping. In my heart I binds to him. He sleeping sound but I with that gal. I gets up and walks outside. I takes in the night sky and thinks bout her. I thinks bout her baby. If they spirits free. If they still in the river or already come back.

His hands hard but his face soft. I wants him all day. When I sorts the tobacco when I sings when I eats when I gets up in the morning when the sun beat down on my neck when my fingers ache with the long day. But I stays away from him. When he come to sleep I turns away. He ask whats vexing me but I shamed to say it. I scared to love anyone. Everybody I ever loves been taken from me.

One night he aint come.

I cant sleeps that night. The babies up crying and me up crying with them. Cora say hush. Got to be a fool crying bout some man she say. Aint I learns you better than that. He out having his fun. Why he want to be in here with you when you aint even talk to him. In my heart I knows she right. But I too scared to say my truth.

When I sees him the next morning he got a feather in his hat.

I gots my knife in my hand.

He aint never look at me. Just come in put his sack down and pick up one them babies. He hold it close to him and sing.

Why you crying little baby. Your mama aint in the fields. This Sunday morning and she gonna come see you.

He rock it like that and sing. He looking at me from the corner where he standing. I sees him looking at my knife. He keep rocking and singing. Knife shaking in my hand. I puts it in my pocket.

I takes you on a Sunday walk he say. Come walk with me in the woods and tell me what you know.

I takes hold the broom. I gonna sweep him out the place. But I sees Cora listening for my answer.

I gots to sweep the yard I says.

You aint got to do nothing gal.

Cora grab the broom from my hand. You go on and see what that fella want.

She take the baby. I does what she say.

We walks to the dancing place. Ashes from the fire still hot.

Last night folks come from all the farms round and some from town Jim say. They want to know what Jim see. I says I sees we gonna be free. And you should see how them people dance. You should of seen us slaves dancing. Mas Watson take the drum away but he cant stop us dancing. We drums with anything we finds.

He please with hisself. I looks at that place and feels how much I miss dancing. Aint been here but once since Mama die. Since I starts working cures. I scared somebody might try and put something on me.

Last time I comes a woman call me out my name. She say I puts something on her man. I aint wants your man I tells her. But she put something on me anyway.

After that I cant lifts myself off my pallet. She put some heaviness on me. Most the time I looks out for myself and nobody can put nothing on me. But that night I been dancing and not paying nobody no mind. Thats when she got me good.

Cora say she my half sister thats why she aint like me. Cause her daddy same as my daddy. Cora fix me up with somebody know a cure. Till this day I never knows what that woman put on me.

That morning with Jim my apron catch on a bramble bush. Jim tease he might as well leave me there with the snakes and the chiggers. Right then we hears a whippoorwill scream. The sound never scare me fore that day but now I plenty scared. Jim take me in his arms and lift me gently off the bush. That sound make me shiver.

Whats wrong with my Sadie. He press me tight.

What you doing here last night. Why you leave me to come here.

I comes here cause folks want me to tell them what I sees.

You aint loss your sight to the river.

For a little while. But now it strong again.

What you see then. I wants to know.

I sees you gonna marry me.

He get a big grin on his face. I laughs. He look hurt.

You hardly grown I says.

Fellas my age already papas. How old I gots to be.

I aint having no babies I says. I aint needs to marry.

You got some other fella you love more than me.

I shakes my head.

Then marry me Sadie. I makes you happy.

What Miss Watson gonna say.

She aint gonna say nothing.

Aint you still belong to her.

I aint belongs to nobody.

Nobody but me.

Thats right.

You know it then.

I knows it fore I comes back. I seen it. I seen you pushing my breath into me when I first comes to my mama.

That aint me. Thats Cora.

I seen you.

From then on I belongs to him. He the one love me so he the one own me. His love good like my mamas. I aint miss her so much now I gots my Jim.

We goes to the woods every Saturday night. Everybody know Jim a seer and folks be waiting for him to come. He look at them real good and say what he see. Maybe he see love. Or maybe he see sickness. Maybe he see a baby or a baby return. Sometime he see somebody gonna be sold away and the people wail cause they aint want what he see. So he tell them they going somewhere better. Or they aint got to worry cause they all be sold together. One time Jim tell a fella he gonna make plenty money to buy hisself and his mama. Jump real high that fella. Kick his feet in the air.

During that time Miss Watsons sister marry behind Mas Watsons back. Man name of Douglas. They living on a hill above town. He got a big place rich in niggers. Folks say they got to get marry thats why they set it up. Old Miss real happy but Mas look sad to lose his daughter. She the one he love.

Miss Watson aint take no fella at all. She stand in the window and look out at the niggers working the fields.

Summer after that Old Miss die. She go to town to visit her new grandbaby and come back carrying the measles. I gives her syrup made from butterfly weed and pepper but she tired and she already turn away from life. They bury her under the sugarberry tree. Grandbaby die too. They bury him next to her.

Now just Miss Watson and her daddy. Mas aint come out the house for a week. Miss come out in a white robe and walk to Lovers Leap to meet Jesus. She climb up there with a bunch of other fool whites so they can fly to heaven. Who knows what happen to the rest of them but she come home alone.

Me and Jim together a lot that fall. Us niggers aint gots to work so hard with Mas grieving. Emma lead the songs and we gets in the harvest. We works and smokes. After the harvest Tailor go to town to see his wife. Nobody tell us nothing.

I knows some the other gals vex cause Jim with me. But aint nothing they can put on me now. Aint no power can pull us apart.

They know that. Thats why one of them take my knife. I pretends not to notice. Acts like that knife aint nothing to me. But when I goes in my pocket I cant feels my mamas hand and my heart hurt.

Cant heals nobody now my knife gone. Folks come to me for help but I cant helps them. Even if the leaves all they need I cant helps them. My power been stole from me. I feels heavy and loss.

Winter come and we burns the fields and turns the soil. I feels a power stirring inside me. I pounds the dry bloodroot to powder. Every night I makes myself a cup of that powder with dandelion tea. When that aint work I tries the spiceberry oil. All winter I sick with cramping. Cant keeps nothing down. Can feels my bones.

The herbs aint working so I tries talking to the baby. Babies like seedlings. If they know what they gonna be put to they aint gonna grow. Not if they gonna be burn or maim. Not if they gonna be chew in somebodys mouth or stuff in somebodys pipe. They wither and die fore they serve that use. If you talk to a baby fore it come and tell it what use it gonna be put to you aint need no root or bark or nothing. Just talk. Children hear you good fore they come into the light. You whisper what the road be like and they aint gonna make the journey. Now if you talk to the baby and tell it the truth and it still want to come aint nothing you can do to stop it. Thats a spirit child.

I dont says nothing to Jim till he feel the round of my belly. By that time spring here. You got me a boy in there he say. Boy with big eyes and big teeth. Big old head gonna hurt when it come out. He say he seen it. He dream it.

That summer I carries the baby right up under my heart. Every time I bends down it bump up against my ribs. Sweat running off my face and I all the time thirsty. Tailor leave me be.

Harvest time come and we works to bring in the crop. I bout to drop. I walking ahead looking for spots on the leaves and thems with curl at the tip. I gots a curve knife to split the stalk. Emma coming behind me with the stick picking up the ones I puts down. Jim loading the sticks in the wagon and driving them to the curing barn. I aint gots time to look for him. They bring us food in the field and we keeps on working. I gets so dizzy I falls out. Emma pull me back up.

You need to eat something she say.

She call one of the children to bring me some corn and water. She watching me close.

Coming your time she say.

I still gots a little while I says. Baby aint drop down.

Whats wrong with you getting big for harvest time. You the one claim you aint having no babies.

I tries to tell her this one coming cause Jim seen it.

You aint nothing but two fools one bigger than the other Emma say. He aint seen a damn thing. You talking like them Africans. If he can see so much how come he cant see his way to freedom. He aint gonna bring you nothing but sorrow. Thats what I sees.

Soon as the barn full they build the fires. Children tending them day and night. So hot up in there one of them boys pass out and they bring him to me. I so tired I can barely stands. The heat of them long days too much for me and I can feels the baby bout to come. I puts my hands on that boy and I feels him getting cold. Jim say aint nothing I can do. Boy aint got no water in him. He dry like a tobacco leaf.

Tailor tell me to make the boy better so he can get back to work. We brings him water but we cant gets it down him. He die the next day.

Day after that my Lizbeth born. She come screaming into the world.

When the harvest finish Mas give us a supper. He gonna marry whoever he say can marry. Jim ask him bout us but

My Jim

Mas say he got another gal in mind for Jim. Jim say he aint gonna marry nobody but me. Mas say he gonna marry who Mas want him to.

Jim come to me in the cabin. He powerful mad. He throw his hat on the ground. Say he aint gonna work for Mas no more. Say he aint gonna work for no white.

I says dont matter what Mas say. He let you jump the broom but he aint giving you no papers. You can marry yourself good as Mas can marry you.

So thats what we done. We marries ourself the next Saturday in the yard. Cora say some words over us and we as much marry as if Mas done it hisself. We jumps the broom under the black walnut tree.

The baby the one marry us Jim say. He change after Lizbeth come. He cant keep his mind on his sorting work. Putting the leaf in the wrong piles. Every day he come home beat. I puts the witch hazel grease on his back. He cry like a baby and let me hold him.

He all the time talk bout running off. I thinks on what Emma say. I aint gonna run with no baby I tells him. And I aint leaving her behind. You promise you aint gonna run without us.

He promise. But he all the way change now. He worry day and night over that baby. More he worry the stronger he get.

While we turning the soil he humming to hisself a little freedom song. Deep river he sing. My home rest over Jordan.

It catch in his throat and he aint want to sing nothing else. We all picks it up. We works sowing the bed till our fingers like icicles. We rubs them to bring the feeling back. I rubs Jims in front the fire. Smoke fill the cabin and the baby coughing. She breathing heavy. That winter heavy on all of us.

Spring come like always and the baby live. She hungry all the time. She feed at Cora and feed at me both.

Mas Watson hire me out to a doctor in town. I says why you gonna make me leave my baby Mas. He say he need the money.

Doc Renard use quinine for everything. He say I aint knows nothing bout healing. My job to clean the place. I gots to boil all the sheets and tools and clean all the blood away. He say medicine too clever for niggers. Say us niggers believes in ghosts and thats why we aint knows nothing. We scared of our own shadows.

He send me to the college to warm up a body. Go first thing in the morning he say. Make it nice and soft so I can cuts it open. He laugh when he say it. He make his eyes big.

I seen lots of dead bodies so I aint scared to do it. But I scared of the college and them young mens. So I goes in the night.

I takes a lantern and walks up the hill to the college. I carries a kettle and some wood for a fire. On my back I gots a bundle of tobacco leaf. I gonna get me some water at the college well and build me a fire to boil the sheets. Then I plans to lay them sheets over that hard cold body till morning come. I gonna keep on boiling them sheets all night long and when Doc get there in the morning his body be warm and waiting.

I does just like I plans with the sheets. I wrings them out with the fire tongs and carries them on a platter. In my pipe I gots some bark from the sassafras root. I smokes it to quiet the smell.

When I gets to the room with the body I puts down my lantern and opens the door real slow. I sees a black man laying on the table. He a old man and black like a African. It make me sick to think bout Doc cutting on him. He got scars all over his body. He already been cut too much. I cant tells how he die or where he from or how come Doc got him here. But I feels for him. And I aint minds being the last one to see him fore Doc cut him up. I gonna wash his body gentle. I gonna wash his old tired feet and sing a mourning song.

I does all that and keeps boiling more water and bringing more sheets. I lays some tobacco leaf on his chest and covers his manhood. Gives him the respect of a elder. I aint never knows my grandpapa and I looks at this man and wonders bout his children. How come they aint bury him. Maybe they far away. Maybe Doc stole a dead man.

Whole room warm and moist with the steam from the sheets. I falls asleep sitting on a stool with my pipe still in my mouth. Close to morning when the spirit come. I feels it touch my arm. When I opens my eyes the old man looking at me.

Make me shiver all over. But I looks back to see if he breathing. Then I gets up and shuts his eyes.

I aint goes back to Doc Renard. I goes home to Clear Creek instead. I tells Mas my story and he dont make me go back. When I gets home Lizbeth walking. She dont know me.

Jims eyes big with tears when he see me. We aint says nothing to each other. Not that morning or that night. He wash me with soapweed to bury the smell of the dead.

Thats a hard season. Everything dark round Clear Creek. Rain falling steady and leaves hanging low. Body turn up in Bird Slough. Body of Nerium Todd. Jim know him from the waterfront. He gone missing close to Christmas. They find him in the water all cut up.

Jim say us niggers gots hard times coming but he aint say when. Just maybe spring a good time to make a move. Baby still small enough to sleep on my back. Mas aint got the money to hire no dogs to come after us.

So we makes our plans. We gonna run to the Stone School. Theys a church that meet there. Jim say they got a hole under the pulpit. A hole for hiding niggers. They gonna help us get to the dentist in Quincy. And then we goes to Canaan.

I worries whether the whites at Stone School aint like the Murrell gang that take away Jims father. And if Jim aint like his father believing in things that white folks tell him. Things that aint true.

Spring come and I cant keeps nothing down. My bleeding never come. I finds some chicory by the side of the road and uses it to settle me down. I aint breathes a word to Jim. This baby gonna be born in Canaan. Aint never gonna be a slave. This baby I gonna keep.

We waits for the night we leaving. Saturday night. All day long we watches and waits. We planning to be halfway to Quincy by Sunday night fore anyone know we gone. That morning I helps Cora with the washing. I wants to hold her close and ask her to come with us. But I cant for fear she say no. She the first one Mas gonna talk to when he realize we aint there.

The clouds getting dark when Miss Watson call for us. She going to Bear Creek to get religion. She want Jim to drive her and she want me to come long to tend a Baptist girl. I looks at Jim and he sweating. But he hitch up the buggy and we gets in. I sits cross from Miss Watson but we aint says anything to each other.

When we gets to Bear Creek Miss Watson tell us to go on in. Dont be scared she say. Niggers come to service before.

Jim got his hat on so he take it off. We listens to the white preacher talk bout hell and the devil in our hearts. We stiff as logs me and Jim. Outside its starting to storm.

After the service Jim drive us over to the house of the Baptist girl. She big with child. All swole up and red. While I rubs her with columbine salve white folks talk bout some slaves trying to sue for they freedom. Any nigger try to take me to court aint gonna live to tell bout it. Thats what they saying.

Miss Watson say Sadie you go tell Jim to put the horse in the stable with the others. We aint gonna make it home tonight. He can sleep in the stable. You go bed down behind the stove.

In the morning trees down from the storm so we goes a different way home. Sun shining bright through the leaves. Air clean of winter smoke. Miss Watson talk to me bout God. I listens and says yes maam. Inside I all tore up. I knows Jim feel the same.

When we gets home Cora standing with the baby. Say Lizbeth been looking for us. Show your mama and daddy how you can wave your hand she say. Lizbeth open and close her little fingers. Jim take her and hold her to him. He kiss Cora on both cheeks.

Our plans ruin for now. Sunday pass slow. Nobody left at the Stone School to show us to the hole and cover us with the pulpit. Nobody to row us cross the river to Quincy.

That night I tells Jim what I hears the white folks at Bear Creek talking bout. He say they talking bout Dred and Harriet. He say all the Baptist slaves talking bout it too. Them St. Louis niggers got some nerve they say. Dressing like white folks and acting like them too.

My Jim

Jim say he believe thats why Miss Watson bring him back from the waterfront. She must of hear tell of slaves running off with abolitionists. Jim say we can makes it to freedom if we can gets ourself onto a steamer. He got a plan. One day when all the white folks falling sick Miss Watson gonna ask us to town. When we gets there he gonna sneak off and talk to his friend loading the steamboats. He gonna find out which one the abolitionists on.

Jim say his friend make good money working the docks. Getting money from abolitionists and taking it from poor niggers he aint never gonna see again. And never gonna claim to know if he do see. Jim say his friend gonna be so rich time he get his own boat to Cairo he aint never gonna have to work again.

We might finds trouble he say. White folks know we the Watsons niggers. But the abolitionists can make up papers saying they owns us. Jim say he gonna wait for a good time when we done with our work and wont be miss. Then we gonna walk over to the docks. We gonna walk separate case of trouble. When his friend point out the whites with our papers Jim come find me in my hiding place under the levee. Then we boards the steamer with papers and new owners. We gets off at Cairo Illinois. Then we free.

I aint so sure bout none of that. Only niggers I knows run off come back dead. But when I looks at Jim and sees him pining for his freedom I knows he need me to believe.

Getting back to the rivers all he can think about. Crossing Jordan.

When he run I gonna runs with him. We leaves Lizbeth with Cora. When we gets our freedom we gonna work to buy our Lizbeth. Cora too. Thats the only way I can thinks on it. Lizbeth think Cora her mama true.

Planting season come and we bides our time. Jim say we aint gonna try the Stone School again cause what happen was a sign. The spirits keeping us safe. Saying go this way not that way. Jim say we gots to listen real close for our spirit guides. They the ones gonna take us to freedom.

We gots our own cabin now but we acts like we aint together. Jim think it cause I mad at him for something or sad bout still being here. But I dont wants him to feel my belly and see how hard it be.

Miss Watson got it in her mind to save our souls. On Saturday after we quits working she gather us for prayer. She bring Preacher Stowe to see who want to be baptize. Who want to be save.

Stowe all the time talking bout heaven. Getting to the other side and resting in the Lord. I so sick with wanting my freedom I cant stands to hear no sermons. Folks all the time singing bout campground. I just wants to lay my head down on Jims chest and never gets up. Nobody to bother us. Thats my heaven.

My Jim

The tobacco aint no taller than my finger when I feels the baby swimming round in my belly. Freedom seem farther and farther off and I aint sure it ever gonna come. I cant gives Mas another baby. Lizbeth safe with Cora. Jim still a young man. He say he already seen his freedom. But he never say he seen mine.

I starts for the woods but I never gets there. I comes to the pond at the edge of the woods. Pond where Jim bring the horses to drink. I takes off my dress. Aint no moon that night. Pond aint deep but its plenty deep for drowning. I climbs down in the water. My whole body shake. I leans back till I feels the water holding me. I just lays there looking at the night. I feels the baby floating inside me. I dips myself under and stays down. It feel free under the water. I comes up laughing. Then I falls back down. I feels my body getting bigger. I gets scared and lets it raise up again. Then I goes under for a long time till I feels the breath leaving me.

Jim find me like that floating.

Whats wrong with you gal.

He wade in the pond and carry me out. I shivers in the night air. He hold me to him.

You gone and loss your mind.

Then he see we gots another child coming. I cant gives Mas another child I sobs. I goes to my grave fore I gives Mas another child.

You hush now he say. Thats Lizbeths child. She ask for him and he gonna come no matter what you do. You aint want to give our baby girl some company. You selfish thats all. Trying to sneak off and get rid of Lizbeths baby. What I gonna say to her when she grow up and ask what happen to her mama. She drown herself cause she aint want to give you some company.

I cries and cries.

We names the baby Jonnie.

Next year the same as before. We sows and plows in winter. Nurses the seedlings long in spring till they ready to be move during rainy season. Topping and suckering in the heat of the summer. Pulling off the worms till time for the harvest and curing. Tired of healing folks just so they can go back to the fields.

Jonnie learn to walk. Lizbeth feeding the chickens. The other children run and play but she all the way watching for the workers. Waiting for us to come in from the fields. Every night she bring me water. I aint gots to tell her. She wash my feet. She comb her daddys hair. Aint but a little thing but she already trying to sew. We gots two children to leave or take. Me and Jim we aint talks no more bout running.

Then Lizbeth take with the fever. I brings her butterfly weed and garlic and five finger root and burr seed. But I worries she aint gonna come through. Cora look after her. I aint trusts myself. If she leave me I be sorrow. If she leave me I be joy. She such a feeling child. I aint wants her to suffer.

Cora take good care of Lizbeth till she can stand on her own. Then she come back to the cabin. She stand in the door her skin gray like ash. Jim tell her to shut the door cause she letting in the cold. But she aint follow him.

He tell her again but she just stand there. Aint say a word.

Jim feeling hard them days. I can tells he all the time thinking bout Nerium Todd. We barely talks to each other. Jonnie teething. He crying all the time. And here Lizbeth acting like she aint know her daddy.

If you make me raise up off this floor he tell her I gonna spank you good. Still she aint do like he say.

Leave her be I says to him. She aint right. She still with the fever. It aint leave her head.

I gonna knock it out her head he say.

But fore he can grab her the winds come up and throw the door shut. Lizbeth never move.

Look to me like she frozen. I gets up and puts my arm round her. I pulls her to me. Her little heart beating like horses being whip. Jim come up on her and yell something in her ear. Then he pick her up and cry.

Thats when we knows she cant hear nothing. That scarlet fever take her hearing. Now all three of us gots tears rolling down our faces.

Jonnie see us crying and he start to bawl. Screaming so loud we starts to laugh. Jim look at Lizbeth. She aint know why we laughing but she smile. You lucky you cant hear your brother cry no more Jim say. She smile at him.

Jim fix his mind on making money. He gonna buy our freedom. Folks give him money for seeing things. You want him to see something you gotta ante up. Put the money in the hat. After a year he got almost fifty dollars. But fifty dollars wont buy you nothing but a half dead nigger. Not even one of Jonnies toes.

I watches my husband sink. We starts laying together again but half the time he turn away. Everything remind him of the freedom he cant have.

One day he in town when they running the hogs to the stockyards. He say them hogs running so fast like they running for they freedom. They slaves being run to market.

White folks picking up and rushing off to California to find them some gold. Jim say he wish Mas go to California. He go to California we go to Canada. They got gold in Canaan true.

All up and down the river folks talking bout Moses. Say she stealing niggers and taking them north. She keep going back but them patrollers never catch her. She make it with whole groups of women and children. If she can make it we makes it. We already north.

My Jim

Cholera strike that summer and Jim take sick. He bring it from town. Mas say we gots to build a sickhouse far cross the field. He put Jim in there. I brings him blackberry leaves and roots and twig tea from the witch hazel. Mas say he dont want me tending to Jim. He buy a old woman for fifty dollars and make her work in there.

We gots yellow fever that winter. And a slave name Ben blame for killing two white children. He hang for all to see. The cholera back again in spring. Jim all right but Jonnie in the sickhouse. In Georgia a white looking gal and her black husband buy they own tickets to freedom. Then we all fugitives. Even if we runs away Mas got the right to cross the border and steal us back.

Mas Stevens slaves dropping one by one. They aint gots no sickhouse to go to. Mas Watson try hard not to lose any of us. He let us kill the chickens for food. And he make his own medicine of hot lemon water and honey for the folks in the sickhouse. He let the mothers come in to nurse and he let the ones with child leave the fields when they sick. Folks say Mas getting old so he aint one to be mean no more.

But one day Cora drop a child and the next day he dead. Mas come to the cabins to find Cora and beat her.

Jim say he gonna lose all his teeth and both his eyes fore he let Mas whip Cora. Jim look at Mas and say it real calm. You aint gonna whip none of us again.

85

Mas Watson turn red as hot coal. What you talking bout nigger.

I telling you what I seen Mas. I seen my death if you touch Cora with that whip.

Mas turn the whip on Jim but Jim dont let him use it. He grab it from Mas hand and strike the ground. Then he throw the whip aside. It lay in the dust like the skin of a snake.

Jim take Mas by the arm and lead him back to the house. Mas shaking but Jim walking real steady. Rest of us turns and walks back to the cabin with Cora. Nobody ever say nothing bout it.

Mas take sick real bad next winter. Cant talk cant walk cant barely breathe. Jim got to lift him out the bed. They bring in the white doctor. Thats how we knows he bad off.

All us niggers pray.

Mas always say he free us when he die. He looking so frail we thinking maybe thats our freedom. Jim say he aint got long.

Time Mas Watson die it snowing. He sick so long nobody figure he ever gonna die. Then one day he gone and Miss Watson crying. We bows our heads when Jim carry him out.

And waits to hear what come of us.

One week after the burial Miss Watson call Tailor to the farmhouse. Theys lots of whites coming and going from the house. Colored folks in the house hearing all kind of talk bout what Mas Watson owe. We scared for ourselves.

Tailor aint come back till late. What yall waiting on me for he say. He look at the ground and spit. Mas Watson aint free nobody but hisself he say. The rest of us gonna be free in hell.

We all sick then. Jim say dont worry whatever happen we gonna be together. He say he seen it. But aint nobody in the cabins sleep that night. Some of us fights all night. Some of us prays and sings.

My Lord he call me by the thunder. The trumpet sound within my soul. I aint gots long to stay here.

In the morning Tailor order us to dust ourself off. Nobody want a dirty nigger he say.

They sell us with the furniture. Folks wailing and moaning. First they sell off the plows and wagons. Then they sell the horses and pigs. We all shivering near the stables. Folks got pee running down they legs. Frost on the ground and we aint gots no shoes. White folks come all bundle up to look at us. Most of them aint got money for slaves. They there for the plates and the silver.

They call us into the curing barn. Less than twenty of us altogether. I clings to my children. Lizbeth cant hear but she know what everybody saying. She holding onto my skirt. Jonnie aint know he bout to be sold. His eyes real dark and big. More white folks than he ever seen.

Miss Watson aint come to the sale. She hide up in the house.

I knows some of them whites cause I done doctors them. I hopes one of them take pity on me and buy me with my family.

We looking everywhere for Jim. Cant finds him nowhere. They selling Mas desk and bed. We next on the block. Thats when I falls to the floor. Jim aint going with us. Miss Watson decide to keep him. A present from her daddy. She got him lock up somewhere till the sale over. Then she gonna take him with her to her sisters place in town.

They carry off the furniture. Now the whole place go quiet.

We gots some fine niggers here. Best in the county. Every one of them sound. Strong and hearty. Mas Watson a good Christian man. He feed his niggers salt pork and let them grow they own greens. First one we got here Emma. She work hard as any man.

Emma cry out when she hear her name.

Mas Stevens come up in the back of the crowd. He sitting on his horse in his high boots.

How much you want for them oxen the farm and all the niggers he say.

Aint a sound in the room when he say that.

Then Emma start to scream. Cora join in moaning. Then all us women wails like we in Africa. Mas Stevens fire his gun.

I gives you twenty thousand dollars he say.

Sold.

My Jim

That night the mourning songs pass from cabin to cabin. Nobody sleep that night. Lizbeth and Jonnie ask me where they daddy. Why he aint here with the rest of us.

He somewhere safe I says. He gonna come and steal us away.

I turns to the wall when I says it. Everywhere the wall patch with black walnut tar. I stares at the wall like I trying to find a way out.

That night my knife come back. Cora the one got it all long.

What you want with my knife I asks her.

You bout to hurt somebody you love. Thats why I takes it she say. That knife for healing. You gonna need that knife where you going. Make sure you put it to good use.

Cora never make it to Mas Stevens place. She die in a fit while the rest of us gathering our things. We buries her in the Watsons graveyard. We hurries to lay the tobacco leaf over her body and covers her with the ground. Jim put two pieces of limestone for a marker.

Folks try to take what little furniture they has. But Mas Stevens say to leave it. We gots everything you need he say. He tell Banes to march us over to his place.

Banes smell of whiskey. Folks say his job to beat us to death and keep Mas Stevens in whiskey. Banes order some of Mas Stevens niggers to burn our cabins. Folks sobbing now. Grown folks sobbing like children to see they cabins burn.

Nancy Rawles

I cant looks. I keeps the fires at my back. I pushes the children on ahead of me. At Mas Stevens place the children toil longside they parents. Nobody watch over them. Lizbeth cry as we walk. She thinking of Cora I spects.

Cora in a better place I says. And soon we gonna be too.

I knows she cant hear me but she take my hand. She all the way try to make me feel better.

Mas Stevens waiting for us on his horse. I scared when I looks at him. I scared of his boots. His boots and his cane. All these years later I still feels that cane pushing me from behind.

I dont wants my children to know I scared so I looks up instead of down when he talk to us. He look at me too. I aint knows if he remember me but I remembers him.

He show us the cabins. You gonna double up he say. That mean he gonna put us in with his niggers. They aint nothing but skin and bones and they looking at us like we makes a good meal. You think you something. You aint nothing now. Thats what they eyes be saying.

The cabins full of holes. Mas Stevens aint give them no paper to patch the holes. He put me and Lizbeth and Jonnie in with his cook.

Mas Stevens cook name Fortune. He say he name her that cause thats what she cost him. She aint know bout cooking and Mas aint give her nothing to cook with. Her real work making babies. She like to be big. Mas let her come in out the fields when she want. Anytime but high summer. She got to work then big or not. So far she give Mas seven children. Soon as they can work Mas sell them off.

One day I asks Fortune why she aint use no herb to keep Mas away from her.

She look at me like I crazy. What I wants to keep Mas away for she say. I owns Mas. I eats Mas alive she say. I takes everything he got then I wipes him away. White the easiest color to wipe away in this world. Easiest thing to get rid of. All you got to do is mix it up with something else. Soon they gonna be more and more of us. And we gonna be the mas and the miss. She laugh when she say it.

I aint laughs with her. If you owns Mas I says why you let him sell all your children away from you.

She mad now. I aint no fool she say. I makes him sell them. What I wants them to stay here for. I makes him feed them and sell them. We eating meat while all you niggers eating cornpone. I makes sure Mas aint sell my children to no traders. They all got to stay near to me. The little ones go to the laundress or the seamstress. When they bigger they go to the factory. Childrens fingers good for rolling them cigars. The big boys work the quarry. The girls hire on in the shops. I sees them at the holiday. They come back and visit they old mama they do. One of these days they gonna come and steal me away. What your children gonna do for you.

I thinks of my children and I shamed. All they got to eat is cornmeal. Anything else got to come from our garden. Mas work us so hard we barely gots time to work for ourselves. I gives my children turnip root and turnip greens. They find berries. Lizbeth catch a fish. But all the time we looking for meat. Mas dont let us keep guns to hunt. And he dont let us keep pigs and chickens. Any meat on the place his. Last nigger kill a chicken had to eat it while it still warm. Head first. Feathers and all.

I looks for the one eye woman I seen when I first comes to Mas Stevens place. I aint sees her nowheres. I figures she long dead. She nothing but bones then. Now I twice as old so she must be twice as dead.

Us slaves from Mas Watsons place works faster and better than the others. But soon we starts to slow down. The work the same but aint nothing to eat. The children so hungry they cry all the time. Then they stop crying altogether. Just moan and bite they lips.

First week on the place Tailor run off. Say he aint gonna work for Mas Stevens and he sure aint gonna work for Banes. He gone a long time fore they find him. When they bring him out the woods he got a wild look in his eye. Banes put him in the stock and whip him till he dead. Even the white folks say Mas Stevens crazy. Killing a nigger he can sell for good money.

I longs for Jim but I aint wants Mas Stevens to catch sight of him. He better off with Miss Watson. She see the value in him. Mas Stevens see the man. He got to beat Jim down till he a boy. Aint no mens work for Mas Stevens. I scared he gonna kill Jim if he come round. Just like he let Banes kill Tailor.

But Jim aint scared. He come to me one night skin all shiny with sweat. He been running like he running from ghosts.

Where Fortune he say.

She sleeping with Mas. Only time she aint sleeping with Mas when she having his baby.

Miss Watson at a camp meeting he say. All the whites over at the camp meeting. Even Mas Stevens. All the good Christian whites and the bad ones too. Some the niggers even there. Hearing bout not sparing the rod. He laugh.

Got his hat in his hand. Inside he got the ball of a ox. Say he come cross the ox in the bramble. He recognize it as Mas Watsons ox. Mas Stevens done half starve it. Jim say if he aint come cross it the ox bleed to death since one of his balls hanging off his hind. Jim take his knife and cut it free. Quick cut to stop the blood. Mud to cover the wound. Then he get a stick and beat the ox back to the farm. But first he let it feed on dandelion greens.

He want me to take the ball and cook it on the fire. If he eat it he get the strength of ten mens.

I aint cooking nothing tonight I says. Cant you see the children already asleep. What you think the smell of meat

gonna do to them. Fore you know it Jonnie gonna be shouting bout his daddy home. And Banes gonna come over here
with his whip. You hush now and lay down.

I makes him a little pallet next to mine but I aint wants him
to touch me. It might hurt too much. Weeks now I aint feels
his touch. Cant stands to feel him for a night then not find
him in the morning.

He honor my wishes but I sees he sad. When he go to
leave I holds onto him. I fears he aint coming back so I starts
to cry. Jim say he better go fore they miss him at the camp
meeting.

He come three more times. Each time he bring us some
meat. He blow on the children and wake them up right fore
he leave. I opens to him again. I weak and I opens. He hold
me like he carrying a seedling. I cries cause I knows I cant
keeps him.

For a long time I aint seen him. Every night I listens for
his whistle. One night my soul heavy like the day he born. I
sees his mama and my mama too. I thinks of his cord under-
neath that white oak. I sees my hand cutting his cord with my
mamas knife. I hides my face.

It raining heavy but I knows in my bones Jim coming to
me. I sends the children to sleep with Emma. They dont
needs to hear the things men and women do when they long
for what they cant keep.

My Jim

Jim come to me with a five cent piece round his neck. Say he took it from some white boys to keep the devil at bay. Say the devil roaming all round Hannibal looking to snatch a nigger like him and sell him down the river. But that coin he tie round his neck gonna keep him tied to them boys in town. So he cant never be sold away from here.

I needs you for my old age I says. Me and the children needs you.

He aint going nowhere he tell me. You got something belong to somebody else they aint gonna let you go till they get it back. Thats why I gots this five cent piece round my neck.

You got my heart belong to me I says.

You aint never gonna lose me he say.

You love that hat more than you love me I says. You sooner part with me than that hat.

He laugh his good strong laugh. I scared one of Mas Stevens niggers might hear us. Then he kiss me and I aint thinking bout them.

If you love me you leave me that hat.

He look at me all serious. That hat aint nothing to me he say. He grab it and run out the door into the rain. Come back with it full up with water. Trying to hold it so he aint spill none but water spilling all over the clean dirt floor.

Now I the one laughing. I aint asks you for no water I says.

But you need some he say. Sitting up in here all hot and bother in front this fire like you aint got no time for your husband. He sure to be beat for coming to see you and you act like he a man free to come and go as he please.

He pull me down to him. But the more he touch me the more I cries. After awhile he fall sleep. I stays awake watching the fire burn itself out.

When the fire go out I gets up and feels for his hat. I all the way wakes him fore the bell sound and fore I light the morning fire. But this time I cant stands to think of him gone and me with nothing of his smell. I takes his hat and cuts a little piece off it with my knife. A three point piece.

I gets the fire going again and lays back down. Fore I knows it the bell ringing. I wakes up in a fright. Jim still at my side.

Banes waiting for him this time. He tie Jim hisself. Jim aint fight.

Jonnie run out into the yard. He going straight for his daddy. I pulls him back and holds him close to me.

What you niggers looking at Banes say. Go on to the fields fore I beats you all.

I makes Lizbeth and Jonnie walk in front of me.

Banes want to hurt him. Say they aint many stripes on Jims back. If you was my nigger I just as soon kill you he say. We hears the whip breaking but we keeps walking.

We aint sees or hears nothing of Jim after that.

My Jim

Every day I worries more. My chest hurt I so lonely for him. The children grow weak cause they aint got they daddy to bring them meat.

One morning Emma wake me up to tell me Jim run off. At first I aint believes it. I knows my Jim. He aint gonna run without coming for me and the children. But Emma say he done run off without us.

Him and me we talks bout running the last time we together. Cant leaves the children with Mas Stevens we says. No telling what gonna happen to them. Jonnie just a little boy but Lizbeth already with the womens. They plenty old to run. So I knows it aint true that Jim gone off without us.

I aint believe it till the patrollers come round. They got they dogs and they looking for Jim.

He been here aint he.

I aint seen him I says.

They throw me on the ground in front of my children.

You lying nigger.

They take out the whip.

I gots nothing to tell you.

They start hitting me.

It raining that day too. Been raining a long time. Round the cabins aint nothing but mud. I laying face down in the mud and the mud feel cool gainst my skin. I thinks of myself face down in the river. Swallow up by them muddy waters.

Jonnie screaming. He grab hold to Emma. I cant sees Lizbeth. She hiding like I all the way tells her to.

They put the dogs on me. They barking and sniffing. I can sees they gums. I covers my head. I cant hears nothing cept the barking in my ears.

Then the gun go off. The patrollers call the dogs back. Mas Stevens come see whats going on.

You leave my nigger lone he say. I takes care of her.

He stamp his cane on the ground.

Two niggers pick me up and drag me to the packhouse. Quiet in there. The tobacco still low in the fields and everything just watching and waiting. They tie me up with a looping stick under my knees.

My arms pull back behind me. My bones stretch long like the limbs on a sycamore. Lord I be pain. And what they doing with my children.

I tries to sleep but its hard to let myself fall away. I thinks I aint never gonna come back. I close my eyes when I cant keeps them open but I aint knows sleep. My throat so parched I cant cries out if I wants to. The blood from the beating sticking to my back. The mud still on my face. I tries to hold on cause I cant leaves my children. Not like this. I wants them to see me strong again.

Days fore they lets me out the packhouse. When they open the door they find me pass out.

My Jim

I comes to in the fields. I scared they already find Jim. And they taking me out so I can sees his shame.

But nobody say nothing bout Jim. They let me out to tend the crop.

My dress stick to my back with blood. My arms aching bout to fall off. Banes push me to go faster. He say I aint seen nothing yet. Lizbeth come with some water. I bends down and I cant gets up. She look at me all sorrowful. She dip her finger in the water and put it to my lips. I casts my eyes down so she know to turn away fore Banes come after her.

That night she put the grease on me and pull the dress off my back. I too weak to scream. It hurt my daughter to see me this way. What kind of life she gonna face now her daddy gone.

I dreams bout dogs. In my dreams I sees Jim running from dogs. He in the woods falling over branches and roots. He falling trying to find his way to the river. He swim the river. The river pull him down and wash him up on one of them islands. The hunters and woodcutters come after him. I wakes up in a sweat with them dogs at my heels.

Jonnie sleeping in the corner. He shaking with a chill so I covers him with my quilt. He stop talking Jonnie. The patrollers been round again. They scare him so bad he cant speak. Like they done cut the tongue out his mouth. Lizbeth aint speak much anymore. So I got two children quiet like the moon. Quiet and hungry like the moon.

Raining again. Maybe they aint find my Jim cause of the rains. I thinks of him with his hat on his head. Or maybe he take it off and use it to catch rainwater. Long as I can thinks of him in that hat I believes he safe and on his way to freedom.

So when they find his hat floating in the river I knows my Jim really dead. Hat cover in mud from the river. Little piece missing.

Jims hat floating in the Mississippi. Thats all the proof anybody need. That nigger drown hisself. Nigger never without his hat. Sooner or later his head gonna come looking for it.

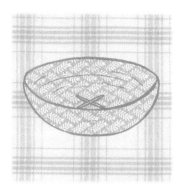

Bowl

See this mark. You can feel it with your fingers. Fore this bowl broke thats the Congo cross. Not a Christian cross. A Congo cross. One line up to the gods one line down to the ancestors in the spirit world. One line over for this life right now and this death too. A circle tying it all together.

My mamas mama a healer. She the first doctor in the family this side the water. When my grandmama give my mama this bowl she know the power in it.

Time they find Jims hat I still gots my bowl. I goes to the woods for some bloodroot. I makes the children eat the seeds. Then I eats whats left. Now that Jim gone Lizbeth and Jonnie all I owns in the world. Something happen to them aint no reason to go on. I scared Mas split us up as punishment. I waits till they finds the body. Then I knows what to do.

Body never come. Not Jims body or the white boys. White folks say Jim must of killed that boy since they both gone missing at the same time. But I knows Jim aint kill no boy less he got good cause. Jim fond of them boys. They pay him in coins and marbles when he tell them what he see.

Nigger under a spell. Thats what the white folks say. That doctoring witch put that nigger under a spell. He a good nigger fore he met up with her. I scared what they gonna do to me.

When Mas hear tell of Jims drowning he come looking for me. He gonna whip me hisself. He call all the slaves in from the fields to watch. He tell Banes to strip me down to my waist. Then they tie my arms to a tree. Not round the tree like usual but over my head. He want me to face him.

Some the womens start to making noises. Mas say they better stop clicking they tongues if they know whats good for them.

He want me to beg him for mercy. He can kill me right there. I just aint wants my children to see it. So after awhile I says please Mas believe me. I tells Jim not to run off. I tries to keep him.

That afternoon Emma tend to me. I tells her to make me a balm from the inside bark of a sycamore. Dress my wounds and lay some tobacco leaves cross my chest. Boil me a blackberry tonic. Emma do everything I says.

Fortune over in the corner moaning. Her pains got her scared this time. I tells Emma to give Fortune some milkweed to make her breathing right. I tells Lizbeth bring my bowl and crush me up some mint.

I wants none of your cure Fortune say. Folks aint want to touch nothing you touch.

None of Mas Stevens slaves trust us come from Mas Watsons. But if we can helps them they work it out of us. Now they scared. Just like the white folks. I looks at Emma. She shaking her head.

Fortune dont survive that baby. Baby take all the breath out of her. Mas give the baby to Emma and tell her to nurse it till he can sell it.

After that Mas Stevens take him a wife. She aint no more than a child. Indian child he call Flesh. Folks say he done stole her off the prairie. She cant talk his language and he make fun of her when she talk her own. I feels sorry for her. Everything Mas Stevens got he done stole.

One day Flesh come to the cabins. I sees the marks on her face where Mas Stevens done beat her.

She got in her hand some leaves. They dry and gray like ash. Where you get them Miss I says. Her eyes full of water and I knows them leaves from wherever she from. She point to my bowl. She want me to take them and pound up a cure.

She want me to put them in my bowl and give them back they power.

I cant helps you Miss I tells her. I aint knows them leaves. You got to hold them in your hands and talk to them in they language. Thats when they give up they secrets.

She press the leaves to her cheek.

A few weeks later Mas take Flesh to town and leave her there. He dont want her no more. I never hears what come of her. Maybe she dead. Maybe she walk home.

After that Mas turn his eye on me. He think up reasons to get me in the house. Take these sheets and wash them he say. I dont wants no trace of that Indian nigger in my house.

I does what he say. Then I goes to the fields.

One night I finds a dead bird in front my cabin. I stands in the yard and calls out my enemies. Nobody come.

Next day Mas ride up on his horse while we topping the tobacco. He tell Banes to work us harder. Then he turn to me.

You cook Sadie dont you.

I keeps my eyes on the ground.

That Fortune dont know bout cooking. And I cant stomach no Indian food. Come cook me some nigger greens Sadie.

I knows nothing bout cooking Mas.

Sure you do. You a doctoring nigger aint you. Come cook me a remedy.

I stays still.

Everybody looking at us. Mas mad now. He tell Banes to take his rope and tie me to one end of it. All the time Banes tying Mas talking.

Maybe theys a little meat in it for you. Your children can use some meat Sadie. And the niggers need they mush.

He run me behind his horse. When we gets to the kitchen he throw me in with the pots and say make the niggers they mush.

I aint cooking without no food I says.

What you think you got in them sacks nigger.

I aint sees nothing but cornmeal Mas. Us niggers we tired of cornmeal.

He strike the bench with his cane.

You gonna eat what I gives you he say.

But I aint gonna cook it I says. I wants to go back to the fields.

We looking at each other now. He gone dark red. I knows he want to kill me right then. But he dont. He just laugh at me.

What you gonna cook then.

You got a garden full of greens I says. We aint hardly gots no greens. And you got all them pigs. Every day we tends them pigs but you aint feed us no pork no ham no bacon no fatback. You sell all them pigs fore you kill one for your niggers.

He turn and leave. I looks for something to steal. But I scared he gonna catch me.

His boots muddy and his face more red. He come back carrying a baby pig by its feet. Pig squealing something awful. He throw it on the block and quick as lightning grab a butcher knife and chop off its head. Blood squirt everywhere staining his pants and the front of my dress.

He cuss and drop the knife.

I puts the water to boil.

For supper the niggers get hog maws and greens but all of them scared to touch the food. They looking at me all curious. They looking at the food like I done put something in it. When they sees my children and Emma eating hunger start talking to they fear. Soon the juice running down they lips.

From then on I cooks. When I aint cooking I works longside the others. Mas got me making him bacon and eggs every morning. He got me making him biscuits and gravy. He say I can puts some bacon crumbs in the mush and a hambone in the greens. But he aint want his niggers getting fat.

I aint wants them to think I good as Mas Watson he say.

I aint says nothing.

We coming on harvest time. Mas Stevens sell one of Fortunes children and use the money to hire harvest workers. They all big and strong black men. We looking better now but we still skinny as all getout. I aint spect any of them working men gonna look twice at one of Mas Stevens gals.

But one of them take a interest in me. Fella name of Nate. He take pleasure in my cooking.

Sadie sure know how to take a little bit of nothing and turn it into something he say.

He work hard but I all the way feels his eyes on me. Sun too hot to think bout nothing.

Once the harvest done and the curing fires burning I asks Mas can I makes a little something extra for the workers. He say make the niggers some biscuits and gravy. He gonna send one of the children to help. He send my Lizbeth.

I aint sees my children much then. When they daddy run off Mas punish us by moving Lizbeth and Jonnie to different cabins. I gots the cabin to myself. After Fortune die they move another gal in there to spy on me. But she move herself out.

I longs for my children. When I sees Lizbeth standing fore me I starts to weep. She put her hand on me. I pats her hair. We works without a word.

Folks almost happy that night. They make a big fire in the yard. The hired men dance. The rest of us too tired and sore to dance. Banes somewhere getting drunk. Mas too. For one night we feels ourselves.

Nate come upon me resting outside my cabin smoking my pipe.

How come you aint with the others he want to know.

They scared of me I says. Scared of the conjure woman.

You aint no conjure woman he say real quiet. You a healer. I hears bout your powers way downriver.

I looks at him. How you know bout me.

Want to walk he say.

I gets up and we goes down to the fields. Moon still bright in the sky. The fields clean and all bare.

When we far away from the cabins Nate turn to me and take my hand. Sadie he say and just look at me.

Your Jim aint dead.

My heart fall down my body.

What you telling me I says.

He look round to make sure nobody near. I seen your Jim he say. He alive as me.

I starts to shake and he take me in his arms. He whisper in my ear.

I comes from down Arkansas way. White folks down there makes a big fight and leave some of them dead. Cant afford to keep all of us after that so they hires out some of us men. I tries to get myself hire onto a farm up this way. Jim give me your name and the name of Mas Stevens. He tell me bout Lizbeth and Jonnie too. It take me awhile but I finds my way here.

How Jim look I asks.

He fine Nate say. Hungry but we feeds him. Traveling with a skinny white boy.

He working I asks.

He hiding Nate say. He tell me he aint belong to the boy.
If white folks catch him they send him back to his miss and
she sell him down the river. Thats why he run off he say.
Cause his miss bout to sell him downriver.

Now I knows why he leave. I cries to hear his name.

Once he get hisself free he coming back for you and the
children Nate say. You wait on him. He gonna come. You aint
got to worry none.

That night I glad to be lone with nobody to tell my heart
to. I lies a long time awake and then I cries myself to sleep.

When Mas come home in the morning he wander over to
my cabin. He knock on the door with his cane and wake me
up. Fore I can lifts myself off the floor he come at me. Fall
down on top of me. I just lays there. He too drunk to do anything. I takes all my strength and rolls him off me. He stum-
ble up. Kick the door open with his boot.

I gets up and stands in the door. I sees some the others
standing in they doors watching. They looks at me and click
they tongues.

I keeps myself to myself. Takes my mamas knife and that
little piece of Jims hat and puts them in my pocket for pro-
tection. I knows my husbands alive. But I aint wants nobody
else to know.

That day Banes aint ring the bell for work. In the quarters
we all lays low. No sign of Mas after he leave my cabin. Folks
say Banes been in a fight. He cut up bad. We all waits to hear.

Mas ring the bell bout noon. He mad when he aint seen his niggers clearing the fields. He call me away from the others.

You come on in here and fix my breakfast.

I makes his eggs. I fries him up some bacon. I starts on the cornmeal mush. Whole time Mas looking at me. My back turned but I feels his eyes on me. Every time I turns round I catches him looking at me. Licking his lips.

He come at me. He back me into a corner and he take me.

After that aint nothing I can do to stop him from coming at me. One day I takes a piece of wood and dip it in the fire. I holds it up in front of me like he the devil. He take his cane and knock it out my hand. He stamp the fire with his boot. Then he take me.

I aint never tells nobody how bad I feels. Who I gonna tell. Fall coming on. I aint seen Jim in a season. Spring when he leave me. But I knows he aint dead. Lord I prays every night he come for us soon.

When Mas come to take me I fights him. Every time he come at me I fights him. I aint belongs to him. I belongs to my Jim. Mas try to break me but he cant. He know he can take me but he cant ever own me. Thats when he turn to my daughter.

Lizbeth cant hear but she see everything. One Sunday I catches her wearing a ribbon in her hair.

Where you get that ribbon from.

She look at the house.

My Jim

Mas give you this ribbon.

She say yes.

Take it out your hair.

But I likes it Mama.

I slaps her hard.

She put her head down. I throws the ribbon in the fire and walks over to the house.

Mas sitting on the porch smoking his cigar.

What you want gal.

Why you give my Lizbeth a ribbon.

She like the bright color.

You stay away from my daughter.

He sit up real straight.

Nothing here belong to you he say. Not even your daughter. Now you on back to the cabins fore I calls Banes to set you straight.

I runs back to the cabins. I takes Lizbeth by the hand and we goes to the woods. I shows her the plants make a person sick. This one give you stomach pains. This one make you dizzy. I puts them in her hands.

Next day when I comes in out the fields to cook Mas his breakfast he say Sadie where your daughter. He order me bring her to him. I acts like I cant hears him.

He say Sadie you can use some help in the kitchen. Bring your Lizbeth in here.

I aint says nothing.

Next day when I comes my Lizbeth already there. I burning mad but I acts like it aint nothing out the ordinary. I gives Lizbeth the basket to go get some eggs. Then I turns to Mas.

If you touch my daughter I says your hand gonna fall off. Your teeth gonna fall out. Then every living part of you gonna fall off till you aint nothing but the memory of flesh.

Bring me my breakfast nigger. Thats all he say.

Every time Mas aint looking I goes out and gathers poison. Foxglove spiceberry pokeberry. Blue iris root. Whatever I can finds. I puts them in my bowl and pounds them to a powder. I tries to remember what my mama learn me. I calls upon the spirits to give me the heart.

I takes that powder and puts it in Mas food little by little. At first he aint notice nothing. Then he say Sadie what you putting in my food. You serving me rotten eggs gal. I swears you trying to poison me.

Working cures all I knows Mas. I aint never poisons nobody. Just something going round.

Well it better not come round here.

All the niggers sick I tells him. I dips my finger in the powder and puts it in my mouth. I wants Mas to see me sick. My eyes feel like they want to pop out my head. My head all dizzy and swole. Something going round.

My Jim

You brings your bowl and work me a cure then he say. Just like you do for the niggers. Cept dont bring me no snakeroot. And I aint gonna chew no black walnut bark.

Mas getting sicker by the day. He holding his stomach and cant hold nothing down. The pain bad now. He double up with it. His tobacco and whiskey all he got. He too sick to bother me. Talking bout calling the white doctor. I scared of what the white doctor say.

You bring them plants in your bowl Mas say. I wants you to crush them where I can sees them. I wants to know what you putting in my cure.

I does like he say. I brings dandelion root and five finger root and root of columbine. I heats up some salt.

When I comes in the room Mas already sleep. I should of killed him all them years ago. Fore me and Jim marries. Fore the children come. After Mama dead and Gwen sold. When I aint got nothing and nobody in the world. Then it aint matter what they do to me. But now I gots my children and I waiting on my Jim. So I gots to kill Mas right this time. So he never come back and they never catch me.

I sets my bowl down on the chair and feels for my knife. I brings it over my head. Knife so small I got to hit him right. I scared I gonna miss. He gonna wake up and kill me. White folks gonna find me with blood on my dress and tear off my arms and legs. Set me on fire.

I sees his cane leaning next to the bed. Cane got more power than leaf or root. I moves closer to it. Many times I tries to draw the power from it. So it gonna break when Mas lean on it. So he gonna fall and break with that cane and his evil be done with me.

I takes the cane in my hand. My skin itch all over. Cane aint nothing but wood and he aint nothing but meat. If I strikes him hard in the head I can kill him with one blow. Then I throws him and his cane in the fire and never looks back.

I picks up the cane. I aint seen Mas wake up. I aint feels him looking at me. Fore I knows it he jump out the bed. I drops the cane.

Pick it up gal. Thats all he say. Give it to me.

I knows he gonna beat me with his cane. When I hands it to him I gets down real low and covers my head. Tucks down low to the floor so he strike my shoulder and back not my neck and head. Waiting to feel that cane cross my back. Waiting to hear it cut cross the air. But that aint the sound I hears. I hears the sound of wood tapping clay. Mas got my bowl in his hand.

I starts to rise. He stop me with his cane. Point it at me like a gun. Like he gonna run it right through me.

No Mas. Please Mas.

He place my bowl on the tip of that cane and spin it.

My Jim

Bowl crash to the ground. I aint sees nothing after that. My hands reaching round like a blind person trying to gather up the pieces and all the time he crushing them under his cane. Under his boots. Till my bowl aint nothing but dust. Nothing but powder on the floor. Cept this one little piece I save all these years.

See that line. That line one day be a circle again. All the spirits cross over gonna come back round.

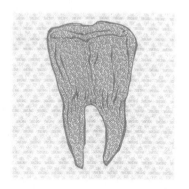

Tooth

Lizbeth got a button. Its something the Widow Douglas give her. The Widow Douglas Miss Watsons sister. Her husband die young and leave her alone on the hill. When Mas Watson die Miss Watson move in with her. Thats where she take my Jim.

Since they believe Jim dead Miss Watson and the Widow Douglas take a good Christian interest in me and the children. They come out in they coach to see us. One day when Mas Stevens drunk they convince him to let them take us to church. Ever since Mas Stevens catch me with his cane he aint want nothing to do with me. He say you can go just so long as I aint gots to come looking for you.

We dress like we going on a picnic. Lizbeth put on her apron. Jonnie tie a rope round his shirt. I wears my head scarf under my straw hat so the holes aint look so bad.

Widow Douglas got a coachman. Old black man with a white beard. He a kind man. Put his hand on Jonnies head like he know how much Jonnie want the touch of a father. He wearing dirty gloves and a red coat. Lizbeth think that coat pretty. She say so. He help us in the coach.

Widow Douglas say thats the red coat of a English soldier. Somebody must of killed him to get it off. See that hole there. Thats the hole from a musket shot.

But Lizbeth aint looking at the hole. She see something shiny like a medal and she reach up to touch it.

Miss Watson say aint that a pretty button.

Lizbeth aint say nothing. She got a big eye for that button. Gold button on a red coat. All the other buttons gone only this one left. Old torn dirty coat. Lizbeth never seen a button so pretty. It hanging by a thread.

Widow tell the coachman give Lizbeth that button. He dont need to wear no button. He dont need to be so proud. Coachman do like she say.

Lizbeth holding that button like it gonna buy her freedom. Widow look at her and shake her head. She give the button to Lizbeth cause she feel sorry for a girl cant hear. Girl just loss her daddy. Girl who always be a slave.

At first I tells Lizbeth throw that button away cause the widow aint mean you no good by it. But then I sees how the child so glad for that button. Maybe the button a charm. Emma say Lizbeth need something to hold. Something she know all the way hers. I lets her keep the button and I aint bothers her bout it none.

Lizbeth pray every night. She learn how to pray fore she loss her hearing and she put her hands together every night. She pray her daddy come home safe and sound. She pray holding onto that button.

Her prayers a comfort to her but they make me want to cry. My comfort in my dreams.

I dreams Jim asleep in my arms. Sometime I holds him. Sometime he hold me.

After Nate tell me bout Jim I wants to tell Lizbeth and Jonnie. Daddys alive. But I dont dares say nothing to nobody.

I dreams Jim walking cross the river.

I dreams Jim swimming cross the sea.

I dreams Jim riding up to heaven but he gone without me.

I starts to hate him. Maybe he got his freedom already and he take another gal. Maybe he in Illinois or Ohio. On his way to Canada. Maybe freedom a starting over place and he aint want nothing from his slavery.

After Mas break my bowl he order me out the house. He aint beat me or let Banes whip me. He just aint pay me no mind no more. I works the fields bending and stooping. Sometime I stands and looks up. Sky the best thing when you trap. Banes tell me go back to work.

I waiting on my Jim like a child wait. Without my bowl I cant thinks bout no cures cant brings down no powers. I done loss the line connecting me to everything.

And Mas got my Lizbeth.

He got her up in the house with him. He got a old woman name Rose doing the cooking. We back to cornmeal every day. When Rose at the cabins or out in the fields I asks her bout my daughter.

She with Mas now.

He forcing her.

He aint got to force her. He just got to feed her.

I aint wants to hear it but I knows it true. Lizbeth seen what I goes through with Mas. She aint got the stomach to fight.

Seem like the longer Jim stay away the less he got to come home to. I starts to wonder if he ever coming back.

Jonnie come to sleep in my cabin. Them folks Mas put him with done put him out. They sleeping all crowded and I sleeping by myself.

Go sleep with that devil done birth you they say. They tell Jonnie all kind of lies bout me. Say I aint no Christian and I going to hell. They in hell and they worrying bout going to hell. Everywhere they look Christians see a black devil. They think God a white mas.

I never makes friends with Mas Stevens slaves but I sings with them. Pass a song down a row of tobacco. Change the line when it get to you. Take up the line somebody give you. Fill it out with one lower or one higher. Speed it up when the work lagging. Slow it down when the night come.

They send Jonnie to me with a bruise face. His eyes big with worry. I tries to touch him and he turn away.

You aint want to see your mama. You scared of me.

He start to cry. He still a little boy.

Whats wrong I says. You look like you seen a ghost.

My tooth hurt he say. They hit me.

His lip swoll and bloody. Open your mouth I says.

He aint want to open it. I brings his head close. Sticks my finger tween his teeth.

He scream and holler.

Shut up I says. And pulls the tooth.

He act like I kicks him in the mouth.

I aint wants you to pull my tooth. I aint wants you to touch me. He yelling like a fool.

Little itty bitty tooth. Next time I slaps it out of you I says. I takes the tooth and wraps it in a cloth.

I aint wants you to bury it he scream. Dog gonna dig it up. Somebody get hold of my tooth and put something on me.

I aint wants no witch to take my tooth. He throw hisself on the floor.

I so hurt I can hardly breathes. Jonnie aint got the heart to look at me.

Go to sleep I says. Aint nothing but a tooth. You think I gonna work something on you. Your own mama. You been listening to fools preaching all that sin. They the ones know evil. They know it like they own children.

Jonnie so small when Mas Stevens buy us. Right away he put to work feeding the pigs and sweeping out the stables. He never complain like the other children. At night he cry in the corner.

Now I gives him the piece of his daddys hat to hold. He smell it and put it on his lips. I shows him how to press it tween his palms and call his daddy back to him.

He hold his mouth where the tooth use to be. I makes him open and show me. He got two rotten teeth.

Clove good for toothache. When children teething I likes to pound a little clove. Put the powder on my finger and stick it in they mouths. But most the time I cant gets clove. Only the bark of a black walnut tree. Jonnie aint like chewing bark but he love the clove.

Mas got some in his pantry. He got all kind of spices and sweet smelling leaves. He mix them with his tobacco. He put some crushed clove in a piece of paper roll it up and smoke it.

My Jim

I goes and stands under the kitchen window. Just stands there looking in. Fall coming on fast. Aint never been so lonely. Lamp casting a soft light. Lizbeth cleaning up. She just a girl but her face getting grown. I stands in the dark watching my child. She up high I down low. She in the light. Starch white apron round her waist. Aint been with Mas but two weeks. Already she look old. Putting on a little flesh. Me and Jonnie skin and bones.

I just waits there till she feel me. All us slaves can feel things. Only now with the freedom folks aint feel nothing.

Lizbeth come to the door. She take my hand and pull me inside. Quick fore Mas can see she say. She grab me and hold me. I stiff she soft. I shakes she hold steady. I aint knows what to say. She put her finger on my lips.

I points to the pantry. We hides there. I goes through them jars till I finds the clove.

Jonnie got a toothache I says.

She make a face. Tear roll down. She miss her Jonnie. Look like she maybe want to tell me something. She aint get the chance.

Mas come in and see me standing in his kitchen with the clove in my hand. I turns round to leave. He come at me with his cane. Push me from behind.

In the morning Banes come to my cabin and take my boy away.

Mas hate me so much. I the only one dont abide him. I all the way fights. I believes he sell my boy cause he want to watch me suffer. But maybe its just for money. He drinking all the crop.

I aint never screams like I do that day. I tear at Banes with my teeth. I fights and kicks. He knock me down. He got Jonnie under his arm. Jonnie trying to grab hold to me.

Others standing in the yard watching. Some turn and go back to they cabins. Banes push me away again. He push me hard. I falls down in the dust. He walking away with my Jonnie under his arm.

I walks round the yard in circles. I tears at my hair and clothes. I takes my knife and starts stabbing at my skin. Only it aint my knife but the shard from my Congo bowl. It leave marks on my skin. White lines like a cross.

Workers starting for the packhouse take up a song. Pass it round the yard. Circle me with it. Song bout hardship. Sometimes I feels like a motherless child. I believes that song the only thing save me from losing my mind.

Thats your Uncle Jonnies tooth.

Pipe

After Mas Stevens take away my Jonnie I aint good for nothing. Cant works cant thinks. Banes come at me with a whip I aint even feels. The others good to me though. They put they hands on me and give me they care. I just like them now. Aint one of Mas Watsons no more. Aint no witch no healer. Just a nigger now. Somebody to buy and sell. Like tobacco or cotton or cane.

I cant sleeps that night. Cant keep my body still. Moving side to side like a body possess. Sounds coming out my mouth like a animal in a trap. Sounds like a bear or a fox. I gots to do something to settle myself. Slaves lose they minds worse than dead. White folks likes to pick at them. Pick at them till they die.

I gots to do something. So I goes to the packhouse. I takes a torch and sets the tobacco hands on fire. For awhile I sits there and watches them burn. Then I puts the torch down and walks back to my cabin.

Folks say I aint knows what I done but I knows plenty. Grief put me out my mind and make me want to hurt Mas like he hurt me. Only way to do that take his child. So I fires the tobacco.

He aint loss much. Fire only burn the outside of the tobacco. The hands rolled so tight the fire cant get inside. The mens and womens come running. They aint nothing but bones but they running to put out Mas fire. Passing the water hand to hand. Fighting the fire with quilts. Children clinging to each other. Turning away from me.

I remembers trying to lift my head. I aint wants to walk with my head down. I wants to look folks in the eye and say thats what I done. Thats me set the fire. Dress tore hair tore eyes burning. Crazy Sadie. I walks with my head up.

I sleeps while the fire burn. I sleeps and waits for Mas. I wakes when I feels his boot on my cheek. I opens my eyes and sees Mas with the cane in his hand.

I tries to lift my head but he push me to the ground. His boot crushing down my cheek. I tries to lifts it off but I aint gots no strength in me. I sees that cane in his hand. I sees that cane and my mind go blank. Pain so bad my mind cant feel it. I sees Jim then. Pain so big it take hold of all the space in my mind. I sees Jim looking down on me. He holding out his hand to me. I puts my hands up. When that cane come down I feels myself in the air with Jims arms round me. Mas Stevens done disappear.

He put out my eye with that cane.

Just one corner of the packhouse burn. When they take me away I standing tied in the back of a wagon. I stands so I can see my work. Only one little opening in the corner of the packhouse. One little sore black circle. Like an eye got a patch. Thats all it cost Mas Stevens. Just one little eye.

It break me sure when Mas sell my Jonnie. Speculator buy him for two hundred dollars. Jonnie so little Mas aint get much for him. I just like that old woman I seen the first time I comes to Mas Stevens place. So thin I can hardly moves. Lizbeth try to give me some meat Mas done throw on the ground. She go down there and get it. My heart all the way break.

Mas spit on the ground when the wagon come to take me. He force open my eye and spit on the ground. He cussing when they take me. Slave aint sound cant fetch a good price. Sellers all the way trying to make a story how we gots that way but whites know they own cruelty. They know you must be trouble to make a white man damage his own property.

You see a one eye person you wonder how that person cry. But one eye do just fine for tears. First night in the slave pen in St. Louis nothing can separate me from my sorrow. I cries all night. Others tell me shush up they trying to sleep. But aint nothing can settle me down. I done loss everything with no hope of being found.

Traders come by the pen. Look us over. Talk bout us like meat.

How much you want for this one. I aint paying good money for a nigger aint sound. These beatdown niggers aint worth all that. Every one I buys I sells but I gots to make a profit. One eye club foot aint make no difference. Damn planters down south snatching up every nigger in sight. The world got to have its cotton its sugar and its rum. But you aint gonna get these prices no sir. Niggers aint worth all that.

It take a week to make a coffle. We waits in the pen till the last one sold.

I waits and waits. I aint working so I feels my tired. Tired like I aint never been. Seem like all them years pressing down on me. I thinks bout that gal use to come to market looking to kiss on Jim. I knows how she feel on her way downriver. Waiting to see whats gonna come of her. Till she got to do something. Cant wait no more.

Us slaves works and waits works and waits. We works for the mas and we waits on freedom. I aint knows if I can waits no more. I waits on Jim. Waits for something good to come. It aint always come in time. Thats what you find in life.

My Jim

Jim come into the yard. My heart see him fore my mind know him. He take one look at me and cry. He aint seen me without my eye.

He left when it just first summer. Now winter in the air. And here he stand without his hat.

Fore he touch me he smile at me. He know I aint want him to see me like this. He lift my chin with his finger and breathe me in. Then he smile at me and touch my cheek.

I cries and cries. He let me lean gainst him.

What happen to your eye he say. Lizbeth aint say nothing bout your eye.

I tells him Mas Stevens take it. He try to take my tears too but I still gots my tears. We cries together. We sits down and cries.

He bring me my things. Lizbeth wrap them all in a rag and Jim bring them to me. My mamas knife. Piece of brown hat. Shard from the Congo bowl. Jonnies tooth.

He bring me a pipe. Good luck pipe he say. Give to me by a boy. Both us spose to be dead. But we both living. I helps him run. He help me run. I loss my pipe. He give me his. Mud from the river in this pipe.

He pick up a twig and clean it for me.

How you got here I says.

I comes on a steamer. I pays my own way.

Where you get the money.

White boy give it to me.

You free now.

I gone to the courthouse for my papers.

How you be free and still in Missouri.

Miss Watson put it in her will.

Miss Watson dead.

She gone a few weeks. Aint you hear.

I cant remembers. Where you going now.

I aint knows. Cant stay here though. Patrollers looking to grab me and put me back in chains.

Why you come to the pen. Aint you worry they snatch you.

I needs you to see me Sadie. I needs you to see how sorry I be. Gots my freedom but I loss my family. What kind a man I be.

He cry good then. I aint mad at him. I aint happy for him. I mostly just jealous and shame for myself. To still be a slave and he free.

I tries to buy you out the pen he say. But they aint sell you to me. Mas Stevens already done sell you to a speculator.

Jim say Mas Stevens act glad to see him. You the nigger of the day now aint you he say. You looking for your family but they aint here. They all gone downriver looking for you. Jim say he like to kill Mas Stevens. But he feel somebodys eyes on him. So he just stare real hard at Mas Steven like he gonna fight him if he say another word. Jim say he willing to

My Jim

die if he can take Mas Stevens with him. Mas Stevens see it in his eyes and walk away.

Lizbeth watching them. When Mas leave she run to her daddy. Tell him me and Jonnie gone. Jim promise he come back for her. Thats a hope I all the way holds onto. Till I gots to give it up.

Me and Jim we just sits after that. We sitting on crates in the yard. Waiting.

I holds my things. I fingers the piece of bowl like a bead. I works it like a stone.

Jim tap the pipe on his leg. He fold it into my hand. He chew his tobacco. I smells him next to me.

He open my hand and spit some tobacco in it. I feels the juice running down my arm. He mash the tobacco with the mud from the pipe.

He working a cure. Take a rag from his pocket. Put the mash tobacco mud in it and wrap it all up. Place it on my eye.

How that feel he say.

That feel better.

You hold that on your eye. I gonna make you something.

He take that little piece from his hat. Jonnies tooth wrap up in there. He take it out and kiss it. Then he put the tooth in my hand.

I watching him work. Holding the rag to my eye and watching him real careful. He aint young no more. Got a beard now. Got marks on his arms where they chain him. Pants too big. Hands like a old man.

He take my knife and poke two little holes in the hat piece. Then he take a string from his pocket. Lick it real good till it small. Push it through the holes.

I takes off the poultice so he can put on my patch. Then he kiss my eye.

I starts to shake. He hold my hand and rub it. We sits there.

He take a little tobacco leaf from his pocket. Stuff it in the pipe. Pick up a stick and put it to the fire. Hand me the pipe to smoke.

But I aint wants no tobacco. Smell make me feel sick. He smoke and I watch him.

Old Finns boy give me this pipe he say. The one they say I kills. His name Huckleberry. Huckleberry Finn.

When Jim say the name I remembers. I seen that boy one day in town. I remembers him cause he aint wearing nothing but a shirt. Like all the slave children. He just a little boy then. Look like he aint belong to nobody. Miss Watson seen me looking at him. Thats Huckleberry she say. Folks call him that cause he live off the wild huckleberry bushes. And scraps people throw they dogs. A shame how some folks live she say. Child aint even got a proper name.

All that a long time ago.

My Jim

Day after Jim come they put me in a gang to go down-river. We chained together. They march us onto the steamer. We one sad group of niggers.

This white lady on the steamer look at us with big sorrowful eyes. I thinks maybe she one of them abolition ladies. Maybe she gonna say something to me. But she never say nothing. I sees her looking at my eye patch. She shake her head and look down.

Folks aint want to look at me no more. I use to be something to look at. Mama always tell me you easy on the eye Sadie. You the devil to deal with but you easy on the eye. Time I could of got any man I wants. White or colored. But I only wants the one.

He standing on the waterfront. Standing in a new green hat. When I last seen my Jim on the levee in St. Louis he tip his hat to me. Thats how I still sees him. Tipping his hat.

Tobacco

Tobacco soft and need care like a person. Doing things gentle so as not to hurt the leaf. Picking off worms like picking off chiggers. Taking care with the leaf. Using it to heal.

Cane dont heal nothing. Sound it make the sound of dryness. Feel like chopping down a straw man. I grabs his throat and slices him up with my long curve blade. Buries his body so it grow back again. Dry body aint got no spirit.

Cane workers got they spirits of cane. Dropping with the heat and tired like stalks of dust. Hard sun beating them down. Overseer yelling sing so nobody want to sing.

I remembers the songs from my tobacco days and I sings them quiet to myself. Deep river. River always the same. Rich black soil along the river banks. Poor black hands turning it over. Sorrow flowing from one end to the other. Juice from the tobacco sorrow and juice from the cane sorrow. Different colors sorrow.

I never likes the taste of cane.

By the time I gets to Louisiana I so dry. Cant feels nothing. All I wants some tobacco. I cries and begs for it. Wants somebody to lay the leaves over me. Wants somebodys hands on me.

I leaves the New Orleans slave mart as the new property of Old Man Cyprien. He the owner of a big sugar plantation in New Roads. Only need one good eye to cut cane. My first day working cane they put me in a gang with a gal bout to drop her baby. She stop and look me full in the face.

That my Sadie she say. She scream.

It Gwen. The friend I never forgets from Clear Creek. The one so good to me after my mama die. We takes up as friends again like we still girls. When her baby come I cuts the cord.

Sometimes you find what you think gone forever.

Old Man Cyprien got bout ninety slaves chopping cane. Half of them talking French. Half of them talking English. Some of them talking Wolof Bambara Ibo Choctaw Spanish. Three of them talking German. Everybody talking Creole. Nobody trust nobody. I aint knows any of the songs they singing. I loss till Gwen claim me.

She show me round. Thats where the sugar process. Thats where they keep the hogsheads. That building the sickhouse. Over there the blacksmith shop. This for the cooper. Here the kitchen. That the laundry. There the nursery. The store at the end of the road. You go there for your rations.

Even in New Roads I still feels tobacco tar sticking to my hands. Cant wash off that feeling even after years. My mama birth me in the shadow of a curing barn and I going to my grave in a blaze of boiling sugarcane. I aint never knows why colored folks scared of hellfire.

They got lots of slave drivers on Old Man Cypriens place. Sitting on horses watching us work. I seen one of them chase a man down till he fall under the horses feet and it crush his head.

We eats rice and beans and cornbread. They feeds us all at the same time when the sun too hot for the drivers. They got us living four to a cabin. They puts me with the Germans.

The Germans each got two sheets and a straw hat and a bag of coffee beans. They sends me to the store for mine.

And thats how I ends up with your mama. The man at the plantation store can tell I the new gal. So he take me in the back and have his way with me. When I sees I gots a child inside me I goes to Gwen for help. There aint no woods any-where I can sees. Only rows and rows of sugarcane.

Gwen say Old Man Cyprien wont have no womens try to do away with they babies. Say he got spies in the cabins checking for roots and leaves. Last gal try to kill her baby got her hand chop off. Aint nothing to do but have it. You aint even gots to love it. Mas gonna take it away soon as it born and put it in the nursery. He dont like to lose no babies. He want all the nigger babies strong. Thats why he buy you Sadie. He only buy us gals good for having babies. He gonna give you some ginger candy when your time come. Then he gonna want you to have another one.

I sick to my stomach every day I carries your mama. I gives birth the following summer. Two midwifes come and tend me. They give me something but I dont knows what. It make the baby come rushing out.

Mas say her name gonna be Elise. I hardly ever sees her till she a big girl ready for the fields. Gwen got a daughter round her age and they friends. They work in the laundry and kitchen till they come to the fields.

Old Man Cyprien like to see a new crop of babies every year. He tell the children he father to all of them. You born on the Cyprien place he say. You from good breeding. You proud to belong to Cyprien.

Mas keep a slave name of Andrew. Andrew got more babies than anybody on the place. He one the Wolof people. He got his own cabin. After Elise Mas put me in with Andrew every fall. He talk to me in Creole. Vien. Reste. Fini. Alle. Thats all he ever say. I has four boys by him. They names Jake Theo Roy Guy. That last one almost kill me.

My Jim

Andrew keep bout his business but he dont father no babies after Guy. He aint got no more power. Folks say Guy the one take it. He the strongest baby of all. Up on his feet fore we knows it. Even Cyprien notice him. Say he gonna follow his father.

Soon after that Andrew loss his cabin to another man. I sees him in the fields and hears how the other mens taunt him. I feels sorry for him. I lets him sleep with me. He just want to rest his head on my chest and tell me his secrets. Say he only ever love one person. A boy name of Lemuel.

Me and Andrew we works and sweats and suffers in the heat. When the war come everything change. Old Man Cyprien aint want no more babies. He trying to sell off the ones he got. He sell my Jake and Theo.

All day and night we labors in the fields. Working for the war. Word come with the soldiers returning from battle. We sees them go marching off and we sees them come limping home. We hears the widows crying. Whole time we working the cane.

We free fore the war over. All us sugar workers up and down the river. We the first ones come under the Union. Troops go from place to place emancipating. Sometimes burning as they go. All us scatters. Sugar fields empty. No more cutting and boiling. No more hogsheads for Old Man Cyprien.

Folks say the world turn upside down when the troops come. White grieving and colored rejoicing. But world turn upside down and we still on the bottom. Guess I gots to keep living just to see when things gonna change.

When freedom finally come I aint feels it right away. They call us up to the house. Troops at the house. Mas in New Orleans. Colored soldier read us a letter bout freedom. Say those of us wants to stay on can stay on for pay. Andrew aint want to hear nothing bout staying. He got a brother live along the Red River. They can gets them a place to farm and work for theyselves. We leaving soon as we wakes up in the morning.

We packs up some food and water and joins the lines moving north. We walks and walks. None of us gots no money to ride the steamer we used to ride as slaves. We free so we gots to walk.

Folks think freedom gonna look one way but it look all kind of ways. Sometime it look like slavery. Folks think freedom something like a button or a tooth. Something you can hold onto aint gonna break. But you can break a button with a tooth and break a tooth with a button. And both of them real easy to lose. Even when you know right where they drop you still gonna look and cant find them. If freedom a place its a place you pass through.

On our walk north we sees all kind of folks worse off than us. Everybody looking for they loss relatives. Everybody looking for work and food. We takes whatever we finds. We been stole away from Africa so we takes what we finds to pay the debt. But thats one debt all the mas can never pay. None of us thinking bout working no more. We through working for the mas. If we goes back to the fields gonna be on land we work for ourself. But that aint the way it turn out.

Me and Andrew and your mama and the two boys start walking north along the river. All the fields sitting idle. Roy and Guy still little. They want to play in the cane. Andrew mad at them but they cant know whats going on. Stay out of them fields he say. You aint a nigger now. They find you by yourself in them fields they think you a orphan. Walk where we can sees you.

Me and your mama aint really knows each other. Now she hold fast to my hand. Shaking like a jackrabbit farther we gets from home. Plantation only home she know. Freedom aint taste like freedom to her. She got to leave her friends. She only have to work the fields during the war. She aint understand what it mean to be own. So she cry when I beats her. She never know hunger till she free. Thats why she wear her freedom like a burden. It scare her more than anything. Most us niggers be happy but scared too. Just roaming round looking for work.

Cept we aint niggers no more. Aint no such thing as niggers now. Nothing but nigger ghosts. Some white folks still call us nigger. Ones cant abide theyselves. They choking on they own filth and still trying to cover us in it. In slavery time we all covered in they filth. But aint no niggers without a mas and no mas without niggers. If you colored you a slave and all colored slaves a nigger thats the world we born into. We still colored but we aint niggers no more. Whites gonna find them some new niggers but aint gonna be us.

You cant trust nobody then. Colored folks as likely to rob you as help you. Some them troops no better. They spose to be protecting us and they whip us like horses. We mostly walking on the road but sometime we goes looking for food. Some the plantations got soldiers guarding they fields. We gots to fish the rivers. When we comes closer north we comes to the woods.

Andrew aint know the woods. His mama talk bout woods in Africa. She living in a village in the woods when slavers come and cut down the trees and steal them away. But Andrew only know the swamp and the cane fields. He know the swamp cause he try to run away to the swamp. He wearing the memory of his capture on his back.

I knows the woods from Missouri. I all the way feels free in the woods when I holding my mamas hand and she telling me the plants. But now I scared in the woods. I scared the dogs will find me there and chase me back into bondage.

But something bout the green like a balm to my soul. Nobody ever tell me but I believes Congo must be green. Not dry like the cane fields green like tobacco leaf. Green like the woods run longside the river. I tells Andrew we needs to leave the road and walk through the woods. That way we finds plenty to eat. Andrew scared but he say yes. He got hisself a gun with only three shots. We eats rabbit that first day. Your mama settle down in the dark and cool of the woods. Andrew find a little stream. We all so thirsty from walking for days in the sun. Andrew dont let us stop and beg for water.

Just when we starts to feeling lucky we runs into trouble. We runs into a slave out hunting. Trying to shoot something for his mas. Them planters taken to the woods. They got they camps set up in there. And they still got they slaves with them. He tell us we better hightail it outta there. Fore they take us captive and make us work.

We leaves the woods and walks along the Black River going north. We makes our way to Catahoula and over to the lake. We aint gots no food so Andrew leave his gun with me and walk up the road to the first farm he see. He talk to a colored man who tell him the boss looking for a stable hand. They call him boss not mas. He give us a contract for a years labor. Me in the mill and Andrew in the stables. It feel just like slave days working from sunup to sundown but the boss aint beat us. He just take away our rations if our work dont please him. We gots us a big garden out back the shack and the boss let us raise chickens. All in all a better life than the cane fields. But when the war over and we gots a chance to work for our ownselves we leaves Catahoula and joins the colored farmers at Smithfield Quarter. Thats where you born.

Best place I ever been. We gots a whole town of colored there. We works hard to make our way in the world. But in the end we aint amounts to much.

Your mama love a boy from Coushatta. Name of Joseph. She meet him in school. Boy with hair red like the river. She say he the smartest one in the school. I never really knows your daddy. He quiet like you. Smart too. Can hears him thinking. Them wheels turning round in his head.

Your mama love school more than anything else but you the end of school for her. Your daddy stay in school. He gonna make something of hisself. Might of been one of them Negro lawyers if he aint in the courthouse that day it burn down. Might be up north now.

You from people love learning. Thats why you this way. Your mama give you all her learning. She learn to read and write in the freedom school. Thats why she aint got no choice but to leave here. White folks cant stand for colored to know they letters. Aint safe for her to stay. Aint safe for you neither. Dont help a little colored gal like you to be too smart. One day they catch up to you and make you pay for your learning. Gotta stay one step ahead of them.

You just a little girl the spring Red River overflow with the blood of one hundred men. Go to Colfax today and you still hear they souls screaming in the flames. Your daddy and Andrew both trap in the courthouse when they lit it on fire. Easter Sunday morning.

The rebels riding high and hollering. Trying to chase away the Republicans. They give us guns to hold off the rebels. Tell us we gots to fight to save Reconstruction.

All us black folks scared. They kill a farmer fixing his fence and we knows they gonna kill us all. We leaves the farms and run to town. Me and Andrew your mama and daddy and your uncles Roy and Guy. We camps near the courthouse. Us and all the other colored families from the countryside. We hoping some law or justice gonna come and protect us. But the courthouse one time a stable. And we nothing but animals running for our lives.

The men send us away fore the fighting start. We hides in the woods but we hears everything. We hears they screams. The horses chasing them to the river. And the ones trap in the courthouse.

Your daddy one the ones run out from the fire. They find his body laying in front the courthouse. Your uncles steal him away in the night and bury him in the woods. He been shot so many times they carry him in a blanket to keep him from falling apart. Andrew we never find no part of. We leaves him in the ashes and runs north. Thats how we gets to Shreveport.

Time I comes to Shreveport I glad to be away from the Mississippi. But this here Red River aint no better. Red with the blood of coloreds and Indians.

For more than a year we lives in the woods outside of town. Some folks scared the whole time. But I finds calm in the woods. I tends the sick ones with leaves and roots. I cares for Papa Duban after he fall sick with the fever. And I saves you from the snakebite. You never cry back then. Just hold your breath. When the troops come back you walk out the woods holding my hand. Papa Duban come out the woods with us. Thats when we starts being a family. We settles in the shanty town once the Union troops come back.

I keeps my things with me. When we living in the woods I hides them in a tree. I takes my power from them. Time I wants to lay down they keep me going. They my shoes. When I gets to heaven gonna put on our shoes. They protects me in this world.

After the war us colored aint wants our children in the fields we wants them in school like the white children. After your mama start to school she aint never want to hear tell bout slavery life. They got to pay us now she say. We aint slaves no more. Them teachers from the north learn her that in school.

But they aint gonna let you get what they aint gonna let you get. Nothing more to it. Even when the coloreds get schools they aint lets us do nothing.

So after all the troops gone home and nothing left but the White League and the Klan your mama decide to leave.

She join a cart of church folks heading west. Say she coming back for you. You cry and reach out for her dress. I turns my head away. Aint used to the sound of you crying. At first I aint knows the sound. Every day you wait for your mama. Round sundown when the workers coming in from the fields you look to see if your mama with them.

Your mama coming back. Just cause you cant sees a person aint mean nothing. They still there. You worry you never gonna find your mama but she gonna come to you. Close your eyes. I bets you see her good.

PART THREE

My Nanna

Cross

*M*y nanna give me this story in the days right after my childhood. After Papa Duban cross to the other side and we lone in our sorrow. She tell me bout the loss ones. She show me them things she keep in her jar. And she learn me to make my first quilt.

Quilt smell like my nanna. Smell like the smoke from her pipe. Like the oil she rub in her hair.

She tell me we gonna lay a cross in the middle. For my mama. Make it like a window. So you can look down into it. We gonna put a leaf in there. A leaf or a root or a flower. Something for the healing.

I misses my mama like yesterday. I still looks for her every day. In my dreams I goes west looking for her. I goes north all the way into Canaan looking for her. But every place I looks she one step beyond.

My nanna close her eyes and feel my face. She move her fingers cross my lips and cheeks. I rubs her hands with a salve made from soapweed and ginger and prickly ash.

My nanna sing deep river and I feels pain like water in my heart. She sing oh freedom and I hears them slaves in the fields longing for the day. She sing coming for to carry me home and I sees the rivers of belle Congo. She sing sometimes I feels like a motherless child and I cries.

Nanna piece the quilt and I helps her. She tell me to draw a hat on some fabric. She want the hat her Jim wear. I cuts a knife and a pipe. And a button for my loss sister. We gonna turn the edges under and sew them things onto my quilt. Wherever I goes in this life I gonna have something of my nanna.

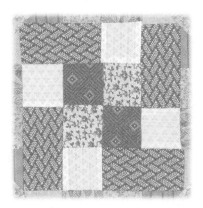

Quilt

ow we ready to make the back. You go get that apron from the high shelf. Thats the apron your mama wear to school. When she find herself with you she put it away. I keeps it for you to wear when you a big schoolgirl. But the colored school been closed a long time and you dont need a apron.

You take that apron and rip it long the seam. I needs some strips bout three fingers wide. You take them overalls from Papa Duban. Cut the parts still got color. Make me a little pile. Then we gonna see what we gots.

Cant piece no quilt without Papa Dubans work clothes. You got you a working man like Papa Duban. Aint scared of work and proud to do it well. Thats the only kind of man worth the price.

See this white line jumping from place to place. Thats your mama. Cant never sit still your mama. Thats the white of the morning sun your mamas favorite time of day. Time to get up and go off to school. I all the way looking at the back of her. Then one day she disappear into the night. Nobody can never keep her. She gonna come back in the moonlight. You wait and see.

I believes I knows where your mama gone. She all the way say she gonna run off to Kansas and follow the ghost of John Brown. I cant says for sure she ever made it to Kansas. Maybe she right cross the line in Texas. Maybe you find her out west.

When you find your mama you still smell that leather on her. Her hands got the dye from the indigo. She got a mole on her chest and one on her cheek. Thats how you know her. She your mama even if she aint know you. You take this quilt and find her. When she see it she know how you suffer for her. You and me both.

We gonna make some wide strips out the blue. Papa Duban never got a new pair of pants. Then right fore he die he got a new pair from the relief. Thats the last relief we gots. When the troops leave most the Yankees go with them. But a few of them stay to help us.

We gonna follow that blue with a brown cause we aint got blue to finish the strip. Your eye need to balance on something. The brown be the bridge. What we missing. Go on and stack that red. I likes what you got going there. Just a little flash of red out the blue.

Might as well puts this old dress to some use. Why I wants to save it. I steals this when a woman aint pay me. I tells her she never give me that dress to wash. It aint on the line and it aint with my ironing. I swears I aint takes it maam. Thats what I tells her. And all the time I wearing it like it mine.

Thats Papa Dubans favorite dress. Once he realize I aint gots it from another man he tell me how much he like it. At first he think I gots it from a white man.

You got to know to watch the white mens. Since the war they act like they cant stand us. Like it aint natural having relations with the colored. Fore the war theys all over us. They still be if you let them.

But you a new kind of gal aint never been used. You still belong to yourself.

Got that button. When you still a girl you finger it whenever you lonely for your mama. But that button aint from your mama. I tells you that your mamas button so you got something to hold onto. That button from my Lizbeth. Go and get Nanna that button. We gonna sew it on your quilt. Thats where we gonna keep it.

I aint gots much longer to keep these bones warm. Dont needs another quilt. Just a few rags to lay under when winter come. Folks living to a hundred but that aint what I wants. You wont see Mama Sadie carrying on at a hundred. I gonna call it a day while I still remembers where I comes from.

This quilt for our loss ones. We puts what we gots left of them here. My Jim. My Jonnie. My Lizbeth. They cover you at night and keep you warm. They colors all here. Brown for Jims hat. Gold for Lizbeths button. Black for Jonnies eyes.

We gots the cross from my mama. Mama Liza. We puts it in a diamond. Thats so you know the Congo cross. Diamond like a circle round it. Different from the cross of Jesus.

This quilt gonna keep you warm. Wherever you go to look for your freedom you take the warm with you. You wrap yourself in it and remember how the old people love you.

The light going now. We gots to stop soon. I can feels a straight line but I cant sees the color. Its so hot I cant thinks bout cooking. Gonna wait for the men to make a barbecue. Maybe fries up a little fish.

Button

You cant really own nothing less you love it. And cant own no love cause you cant never catch it.

The wars over long time ago but I still aint tastes my freedom. You meet colored folks living to be a hundred and twelve. White folks say we must gots it good if we living to be a hundred and twelve. But we just trying to live till our freedom thats all.

I gots from my mama a few things. She give me a bowl belong to her mama and she give me her knife. She learn me how to find roots and leaves in the woods. How to put them in that bowl and crush them up. How to use just the right amount. You aint want to kill folks Sadie. You want to cure folks she say. But times I aint so sure.

When I cant goes no farther knife call me with her comfort. I helps you any time it say. I helps you escape from this place. But I cant brings myself to answer. Times keep getting worse. And I keeps hoping they gonna get better.

The worse they get the more I remembers. Too old now to recall all the times from being young. But I remembers what I aint sees no more. I remembers my husband and children. You know how I done prize Papa Duban. But he aint never take the place of my Jim. It make me sad every time I numbers my loss.

Jim and me we makes our plans. Whoever gets to freedom first gonna find the other. I all the way knows him no matter how he change. I knows him by the scar on his chin. And the drumming in my chest.

I cant tells you much bout love. I cant tells you where to find it. When we colored gots a price on our heads some white folks treat us better than they do today. Looking to keep us down every chance they get. Specially the colored mens and womens want something better for theyselves.

After Jim I thinks nobody gonna ever loves me again. But Andrew love me in his way. And Papa Duban love me. And my children love me. And you Marianne Libre.

I the one who loss how to love. I tries to love Papa Duban. He a good man him. I tries to love my children.

Your mama Elise. And all them boys born of the cane. But I never shows nobody my first heart. They never seen the heart I borns with. It die a long time ago back in Missouri. Back in the slave pen in St. Louis. Last time I sees my Jim.

I aint never knows how Jim find me in Shreveport. Many times I dreams he gonna find me. After the war lots of folks go looking for they kin. But I stays with Duban and tries to make the best of things. I aint wants to leave your mama and uncles. I aint never gonna leave no children again. I knows if I stays put my Jim gonna find me.

One day I comes back to the cabin and he there.

I looking for Miss Sadie Watson he say. They tell me I can finds her here. He wearing a new hat.

My heart stop. I barely gots a breath in me.

He aint sound no different to me. Same big laugh.

Who come asking bout somebody no longer living I says. I aint smiles or nothing.

He grab me with his big hands and I starts to cry. I feels for the scar on his chin.

It me Sadie. Your Jim. Aint you know me. Been twenty years since I holds you. But I never gives you up.

You come back to me Jim. At last you come. I leans into him. But when he try to kiss me I turns away. I gots a husband now I say. Name of Duban. He working in the foundry. And thats my grandbaby in the corner. She sick with the fever and I comes home to check on her. I needs to get back fore they miss me in the fields.

How old that little one he say. Cant be no more than two. He take you in his arms and lift you to his cheek.

She four I says but she aint got no meat on her.

They tell us we free he say but we still aint gots no meat. He pull a piece of salt pork from a rag in his pocket. He hold it to your mouth and let you suck on it. You aint got strength to bite it. He rock you in his arms.

I cant leaves her I says. Her mama aint got long here. Me and Duban all she got. I leaves my firstborn child long years ago on Stevens farm. You know what come of her.

He put you down and hang his head.

Our Lizbeth gone he say. After they take you away I runs to the territories. It aint safe for me in Hannibal. Them slavers put a bounty on my head. So I runs west. But I comes to find our Lizbeth soon as I hears the Union in Hannibal. She with the refugees. Small and frail and weak. She ask me bout her mama. I aint knows what to say. So I tells her I seen you with my sight. I seen you just like today. And I knows you still alive. But her heart broken and she die in the refugee camp. Next day I comes and she aint there.

I cries out to hear it. He hold onto me.

She ask me to give you something he say. He pull that gold button out his pocket. I fingers it and cries. We both gots tears falling everywhere. Ears nose cheeks chin we weeps into each other.

What bout our Jonnie. I whispers his name.

I aint never finds what happen to Jonnie he say. Mas Stevens sell him to the slave traders and they carries him off to Mississippi. I talks to a fella from Greenville say he work with a Jonnie in the delta. Over there in Sherard. But I goes there asking round and nobody can call him. Must of been some other Jonnie born Missouri way. I aint knows what name he go under nowaday. He might not remember the Watson place.

I changes my name but you still finds me.

Folks know you by your eye he say. Aint Sadie they say. Sallie. Hannibal Sallie.

I been all kind of people since you seen me last. Aint wants to talk bout that now. Them days on the Watson place a long time gone but seeing you brings them back. Them days when we both young and free with ourselves.

He look sad when I says that. We marries for all time he say. Aint you remember the day. You say you mine forever. Under a black walnut tree. I walks so far to find you. Now come away with me. We carries that baby girl with us. And settles wherever we wants. I builds you a house with windows. Next to a black walnut tree.

Jimmy you know I loves you. Loves you from the moment you born. I waits all my nights for the day when you come back to me. But now I gots another. I gots two sons and a daughter living and none of them Dubans. But he father them all and my granbabies too. So him I cant thinks of leaving.

You break my heart sweet Sadie. I comes across the years to find you. I always waits for you.

I knows you got a woman waiting. Goodlooking man like you. I believes you seeing a younger gal. Under a black walnut tree.

Dont tease me now Sadie. I aint gots no woman but you. You say you love another but I cant says the same is true. I gonna take my hat and wanders till I finds another home. When I finds it I writes you a letter so you know where your Jim done gone. So gal dont fry me no fritters dont take me in your arms. I cant stands to think of leaving when we free to do as we wants.

Only ones free the spirits I says.

Then I gonna see my Sadie in heaven for sure. He turn real sad to go. I gives him a kiss on the back of his neck. I aint never seen him no more.

Now that Duban gone I keeps thinking Jim gonna come back my way. I never gets no letter from him. But my heart know he alive. It sing for him.

Guess I gonna be in heaven fore I sees my Jim. Gonna greet the good Lord fore I holds him again. Guess I gonna be an angel fore the light of his smile touches my face one more time.

My Jim

When he leave he take all the light with him. But every time I thinks on him the light come back.

Lets put up this quilt and look at it. You call off what you see. I believes we gots everybody up there. Thats Papa Duban surrounding everybody protecting us like in life. And your mama close up next to him following him down the road. That red for your daddy. Red what they calls him. And that yellow dress I wears into the ground. How it look now in your quilt. You take Lizbeths button and sew it on there. Black for Jonnies eyes. Brown for Jims hat. All them watching over you. Folks you aint even know wishing you well praying right now for your soul. If you let the spirits near you they guide you along. All them Africans. They spirits never settle till the last of they children come home.

Everybody who love come back. Sooner or later they come for you. You feel they hand on your shoulder. Or they spirits in the room with you. Some sitting quiet some raging. Settling over you like dust. Sometimes it they voice that come. They fingers pulling your hair in the night.

I gives you my first heart Marianne. The heart I gots for my mama. And the heart I gots for my Jim. You show me my heart again when you ask me bout my things. Theys spirits in things.

You take that quilt wherever you go. When you old and wore you think on me and all the others love you. You close your eyes and feel our love coming up behind you. Thats all you got in this world.

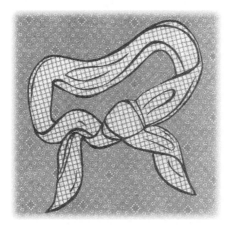

ACKNOWLEDGMENTS

My Jim was a difficult book to write. Fortunately I had much help from spirits, angels, scholars, and artists.

MY SPIRITS

My first debt is to my ancestors, to the ones who endured and the ones who did not, to the ones who wrought good and the ones who did not. As a writer, I am grateful for their stories, even the painful ones.

In order to find an approach to writing this novel, I revisited the nineteenth-century slave narratives by luminaries such as Frederick Douglass, Olauduh Equiano, William and Ellen Craft, and Harriet Jacobs and scoured the histories of former slaves recorded by artists, writers, photographers,

Acknowledgments

and social scientists in the 1920s, '30s, and '40s, a group of scholars that included Zora Neale Hurston. In addition to those who lived these stories and brought them to the light, I owe a debt to historians such as Arna Bontemps who would not let them die. I came to love these penultimate American stories due to the passion of teachers who insisted I read them.

I join those around the world who seek to end the brutal practice of holding bodies captive, starving spirits, and stealing labor. I honor past, present, and future guardians of human rights for recording, publishing, and broadcasting the worst of human deeds and for working so passionately to bring an end to them. From Sojourner Truth and Henry Highland Garnett to Fannie Lou Hamer and Bob Moses, from Tecumseh and Adario to César Chavez and Dolores Huerta, from Anti-Slavery International and the American Friends Service Committee to Human Rights Watch and Médecins sans Frontières, I take my inspiration.

MY ANGELS

I doubt this project would have succeeded without the tremendous support I received from angels at every step along the way.

For her infectious belief in my creative endeavors, Robin Rawles is without peer. If not for her, I would not be.

Acknowledgments

My Jim could not have been conceived without the loving kindness of Martine and Nadine Pierre-Louis, who gave of their considerable wisdom and talents. Thank you to Nadine for her help with lyrics and her ideas for the presentation of the book.

For her support and enthusiasm the whole way through, I thank Marla Durden. Our meetings sustained me through difficult times and joyous ones as well.

If not for the love and generosity of Sheila Arthur, I don't know that *My Jim* would have seen the light of day. From crucial help with research and organization to project development and documentation, at no stage did I lack for brilliant and insightful companionship.

Writing partner Barbara Thomas helped me, as always, to put my work in context and to rethink my life as an artist.

Tim Noonan is an angel for many. I am blessed that he occasionally visits me, as I am grateful for the faith of all the Noonans.

Cheryl Alexander lent her invaluable support, superior knowledge, and enduring friendship.

Lois Finzel donated her compassion and intelligence, along with her tremendous integrity.

For lending her poet's eye, keen mind, and open heart, I am ever grateful to Kathryn Ritchie, who convinced me that the difference between red and maroon is no trivial matter and that I need to recheck my facts and mind my words for the many readers more learned than I.

Acknowledgments

Thank you to writer and teacher Linda Brown for reading an early draft of *My Jim* and for sending me her spirited comments, especially *"My Jim* better be *Our Jim."*

For their early and enthusiastic support for the idea of *My Jim*, I am indebted to Jim Baum, Kathy Lusher, Karen McFarland, Amanda Mecke, Dave Mosley, and Jane Schwab.

For important and timely support as the project developed, I thank Anna Balint, Kay Dendy, Nancy Emery, Lisa Montgomery, Patricia Picou-Green, Niki Riley, and Dee Thierry.

Thank you to Lorine Huffman for her memories of tobacco farming and to Whittnee Chen for putting me in touch with her beloved Great, not to mention her fabulous book club.

Joyce and Clay Dennison, Nicki Edson, and Anne Mulherkar provided me with opportunities to talk to important people about important things. The thoughtful and inquisitive gathering of writers and readers at Allied Arts in Yakima did much to encourage and challenge me, as did the Conversations on Race Book Club at St. Thérèse Catholic Church in Seattle and the students, teachers, and staff of the Powerful Writers Program.

Carmen Ufret-Vincenty, Leah Bui, Laurie Rostad, and their families helped me tend to my most important work. I am hugely indebted, especially to the Santana family. Life is

Acknowledgments

made richer by Maple. Thank you to all the angels who hang around that place.

Dr. Allen-Agbro and Dr. Pierre-Louis tended to body and spirit during a vulnerable time. I am enormously grateful to the two of them and to all the doctors who shared their deep wisdom about the essence of words and beings: Christine Coe, Anne Ganley, Cathy Johnson, Jason LaChance, Frank Lioe, Jennifer Melville, Libby Parsinen, Marion Winniers, and Joseph Zimmer.

As always, I have been greatly aided in my efforts by the love of the Rawles and Domingue families in Los Angeles, the Rawls of Chicago, and the Pierre-Louis and Guenneguez families in Seattle. They bolstered me at just the right moments, as did longtime friends Teri Lewis, Kayoko Miyagi, Mary Ellen O'Connell, and Maureen Sweeney. A special note of thanks goes to my community of artists and friends on Lopez and Waldron Islands and in Yakima and Bellingham.

MY SCHOLARS

Information about slavery, past and present, is readily available from the Library of Congress, the Moorland-Spingarn Research Center at Howard University, the New York Public Library's Schomburg Center for Research in Black Culture,

Acknowledgments

the New Press, PBS, NPR, HBO, BBC, the National Geographic Society, the Smithsonian Museums, university presses, children's books, and everywhere you look.

New scholarship emerging about the lives of individual American slaves makes it possible to trace names and stories that had been hidden from view. In May 2002, two months after I got the idea for *My Jim,* I was fortunate enough to attend a conference on slavery at the University of Washington. I owe a debt of gratitude to Stephanie Camp and to all the brilliant historians who presented there.

I would have been lacking in confidence without the support of historian Sharla M. Fett, whose book *Working Cures: Healing, Health, and Power on Southern Slave Plantations* was of enormous help to me. Her belief in *My Jim* lifted me, and I am most grateful for her thoughtful reading of the manuscript.

I wanted *My Jim* to follow history as closely as fictionally possible. Along the way, I was inspired and educated by the works of many exceptional scholars. Works by historians Sterling Stuckey, Gwendolyn Midlo Hall, Quintard Taylor, Andrew Ward, Ted Tunnell, and Ron Powers were especially important to me.

I am grateful to Alan Miller and Leorah Abouav-Zilberman at Berkeley High School for their willingness to teach *My Jim* to their students. I am awed by all the preparation and scholarship involved in their work.

Acknowledgments

It was by presenting notes and sketches of *My Jim* to Sue Broder's students at John Muir in Seattle that I came to realize how the stories of slaves engage the minds and hearts of children everywhere. To those brave students and all the others who have taught me so much about life over the years, I hope this book can begin to repay you.

To the first scholars in my life, Ann Marie and Manfred Rawles, I owe a tremendous love of knowledge and an unwavering faith in my own opinions, which some would say is unwarranted. Of course, they would be wrong.

Of all the wonderful scholars who have influenced me on my writer's journey, Evaline Kruse was the foremost. I also acknowledge the exquisite influence of Steve Carter, C. Bernard Jackson, Linda Walsh Jenkins, Ursula K. LeGuin, and Freddy Paine.

MY ARTISTS

Tina Hoggatt read the first draft of *My Jim* and offered her criticism and support. For her brilliant vision of the art for *My Jim*, I am ever in her debt. *My Jim* was conceived as an illustrated book but I had no power to make that happen. It was Tina who made the quilt a reality. She could not have done so without the accomplished hands of Nancy Gibson, Ann Milliam, and Cynthia Milliam. Thank you to Jim Watkins and Carl Beck for leading us to their genius. Thanks

Acknowledgments

to Marilyn McCormick for sharing her expertise and to Bernetta Branch for imagining the beautiful backing and working to bring it all together.

This project owes a debt to the master quilters of Gees Bend, Alabama, whose work helped me envision a grandmother telling her granddaughter a story as they shared the intimacy of quiltmaking. At the time I was completing the first draft of *My Jim*, the Whitney Museum's marvelous exhibition "The Quilts of Gees Bend" was sending art lovers across the country into states of ecstatic discovery. I benefited greatly from the stories of love and art that have come to us from these remarkable women.

Visual artists Alicia Galindo, Daniel Minter, Lyn McCracken, John Mifsud, Maureen O'Neill, Kim Powell, Sudeshna Sengupta, Jim Smith, Barbara Earl Thomas, and Inye Wokoma blessed me with their amazing creations. Thank you to Maureen for her magnanimous spirit, which guided me to Cathy and Jim. A special note of thanks to Hugh Kenny. Love and thanks to Monica Spooner-Jordan for her faith and prayers and for bringing us Sadie.

While writing *My Jim*, the rhythms of traditional American music were in my ears. Original music found its way into the studio through the grace of Edree Allen-Agbro, Scott Bartlett, Carlene Brown, Mark Broyard, Dennis Cahill, Robert Louis Cooper, Felicia Loud, Ellen Finn, Hilliard Greene, Charles Hiestand, Julie Mainstone, Stephen Michael

Acknowledgments

Newby, Venise Jones-Poole, Cathy Sims, Larry Sims, and Laura Wall.

Thank you to Carletta Carrington Wilson for sharing with us her powerfully evocative poem, "Alphabet of the Captured." A special thank you to Nadine and Veronica for their thoughtful interview.

My strong feeling that *My Jim* needed actors to bring it to life was heard, received, and fulfilled by Valerie Curtis-Newton, who I consider to be one of the finest talents in American theater. I was fortunate to have the enthusiastic support of all those involved with the Hansberry Project at ACT Theatre in Seattle. I am particularly grateful for the dynamism that Vivian Phillips and Susan Trapnell bring to their every endeavor.

Important project support came from Artist Trust, the Central District Forum for Arts and Ideas, Jack Straw Productions, the Seattle Office of Cultural Resources, and the Walter Chapin Simpson Center for the Humanities. Elliott Bay Book Company lent hands and hearts to this effort, as did Book It Repertory Theatre and Langston Hughes Cultural Arts Center. I am grateful to everyone who helped me get the word out.

When care is taken with books, authors, and ideas, publishing pays tribute to its origins in the book arts. I am most

Acknowledgments

grateful to Crown Publishers for taking on this project. I acknowledge all the people who worked on *My Jim*, especially Christopher Jackson. His elegant goodness, his knowledge of history and literature, his mile-a-minute brain were all I could have asked for. Much gratitude is owed to Genoveva Llosa for trying to keep track of Chris and for helping to shepherd this manuscript through production.

Victoria Sanders of Victoria Sanders & Associates was my guide from the beginning. I thank her and Di Ann for their enthusiasm, savoir-faire, and continuing belief in all things good. Thanks to Imani Wilson for lending her considerable influence during those crucial early days and to Benee Knauer for sorting us all out.

Continuous blessings to all the good folks who helped me in Hannibal, especially Richard and Diane Hammon of the Stone School Inn Bed & Breakfast. Richard's sourdough pancakes and enthusiasm for local history were a rare treat.

Lastly, I am indebted to Samuel Clemens, without whom this work would have been unthinkable.

Nancy Rawles, July 2004

ABOUT THE AUTHOR

NANCY RAWLES enjoys teaching history to children. Her novel *Love Like Gumbo* won an American Book Award from the Before Columbus Foundation, and her novel *Crawfish Dreams* was selected for the Barnes & Noble Discover Great New Writers Program. She lives in Seattle.